When Asher Smith, huntsman to the
Belstone pack, first saw Tag, he was a
tiny, helpless fox-cub, close to death.
But Tag survived, and grew healthy
and strong, reared in a litter of hound
puppies. A close friendship developed
between the cub and Merlin, one of
the litter. When the two grown
animals separated, Merlin became the
best hound in the pack, and Tag
became famous as "The Fox They
Cannot Catch"...

"It is an extraordinary story, and
utterly realistic. The book evokes
the thrill, the agony, and the horror
of fox-hunting with immense
descriptive power, and I found it a
shattering read."

—*Sunday Express*

FREE SPIRIT

David Rook

Originally published as
"The Ballad of the Belstone Fox"

A BERKLEY MEDALLION BOOK
published by
BERKLEY PUBLISHING CORPORATION

Originally published in Great Britain
under the title
The Ballad of the Belstone Fox
by Hodder and Stoughton Ltd.

First American Edition, 1978.

SBN 425-03728-2

BERKLEY MEDALLION BOOKS are published by
Berkley Publishing Corporation
200 Madison Avenue
New York, N.Y. 10016

BERKLEY MEDALLION BOOK ® TM 757,375

Printed in the United States of America

Berkley Medallion Edition, FEBRUARY, 1978

Dedicated to
Bernard and Giselle Kearley
with affection and gratitude

Chapter One

As Tod ENTERED the stillness of Kennel Wood it was hardly ten o'clock, yet already the moon was casting shadows across the earth. Although there was no wind, the twigs at the tops of the trees were moving gently—as if the trees themselves were breathing; faintly yet, but with a gathering strength and sureness as winter became more and more a memory.

Tod pulled the collar of his old overcoat closer round his throat; he was over seventy and his blood ran cold at night, even in the summer. He walked with a long, shambling stride that could carry him across miles of rough country without fatigue. As he penetrated farther into the depths of the wood, it became darker; the moonlight was being soaked up by the dense mass of twigs long before it reached the ground, and only stray shafts hung against the velvet blackness. Brambles pulled at his baggy corduroy trousers, already scarred and patched, but he did not notice them.

He entered the heart of the sleeping wood. Here the trunks rose, smooth and massive for a full seventy feet before the first great boughs flared suddenly from the central columns. Beneath the roof of interlocked branches the floor of the wood was smooth and free of undergrowth; the indistinct shape of the old man blew across the spaces between the trees like a leaf. Tod loved this part of the wood, and feared it, too.

Later he left the ancient stillness and walked out of the shadows into a clearing which nestled like a lake of moonlight in the dark mass of trees. Here he looked up at the sky, gazing at the stars and the drifting clouds; he was still standing there five minutes later when he first noticed the sound . . . It was so faint that Tod was not certain he hadn't imagined it, until he heard it again. He stood like a pointer, his head thrust towards the source of the sound. It came again, almost inaudible; a little forlorn cry, a fragment of fear or pain, or both. He walked forward slowly and stopped after thirty yards to listen; nearer, this time. He moved on again, a little to his left, and stopped; silence. He waited for a long time before he heard it again, and when he did, it was almost at his feet. In front of him a bush cast a pool of shadow on the tangled grass. He looked at it, trying to pierce the dimness with his old eyes, but saw nothing—then a movement. He knelt and reached into the shadow; his hands found and closed on something small, furry, damp to the touch, and just—only just—alive.

Chapter Two

ASHER SETTLED DOWN in his comfortable, over-stuffed chair and stretched his legs out appreciatively. He watched the flickering log fire reflected down the length of his top boots and pulled at the stiff material of his stock, knowing that it would go on chafing his throat until that delicious moment when he would undo studs and pins and pull it off before climbing into a hot bath ... he jumped perceptibly as John Kendrick slapped the leather-bound arm of his old club-chair—the twin of the one in which Asher was sitting, placed on the other side of the big fireplace.

"Here it is," Kendrick exclaimed, with a note of triumph in his voice; "I told you!"

He got up stiffly and stumped across to Asher, holding the book out in front of him, open at the relevant entry, Asher leaned forward and looked, while Kendrick grinned down at him, anticipating the huntsman's concession of defeat. Asher looked up.

"You're right, sir," he said, in his slow, soft way, "Forester it is."

"Ha!" Kendrick snorted, then turned and went back to his armchair, speaking as he went:

"Forester '47—and the only reason I knew that is because I had to look up old Ardent's line the other night, and she traces her heritage back to him."

Asher was still smiling his lazy smile, his teeth

showing white against the weathered mahogany of his face.

"I shan't take you on again in a hurry," he said.

Kendrick laughed—a short savage bark.

"You're an old hypocrite, Ash," he said.

The whole thing was a ritual, and both men knew it; John Kendrick, Master of the Belstone Hunt, and Asher Smith, his huntsman. The Belstone hunted three days a week, and three evenings a week, all through the winter; Master and huntsman met in the panelled warmth of the study to talk over the day's happenings. It was part of the ritual that they still wore their breeches and boots, as though prolonging the discomfort so as to heighten the pleasure of getting out of the confining things later on.

With their legs stuck out towards the fire, they would discuss the day's events as an *hors-d'oeuvre* before the main course: the hounds. Then they would settle a little deeper into their armchairs and start talking about mystical abstractions like "nose" and "drive" and "substance"; then the character and performance of individual animals; then breeding— the never ending pursuit of perfection; and almost everything they said had been said before, many times, and even this they loved: the saying again of mellow, well-worn words, following tried and trusted paths of thought, like a favorite walk through the gardens. And Kendrick getting up stiffly from the depths of his leather armchair, limping three strides to the bookcase, reaching up and taking one of the line of uniform morocco-bound volumes, then limping three strides back to his chair, settling back with a sigh . . . then the pages turning, the orderly sections and sub-sections, the diagrammatic pedigrees, and at last Kendrick stabbing down with his stubby finger before settling some disputed point or other—about who traced back to whom, or what year did we have the good draft from the Belvoir, or how many seasons did Ringwood hunt...that sort of argument. And sometimes there would be a companionable silence, and Asher would look around the room at its paneling and its wall full of books: he would see the firelight reflected in the painting by Cuyp that hung over the desk and then he would touch the old leather of the armchair in which he sat, and the mosaic inlay of the table at his side—sitting silently and safely in the welcoming room...

By the time Asher got back to the kennels, the moon was up. He walked past the front of the house and round to the side-door that opened on to the lodging rooms and yards. The hounds heard his footsteps and knew him immediately; all movement ceased and they waited for him, frozen in any position, skin prickling with the excitement that his presence always created. He opened a heavy door and walked across the court, which shone wet in the moonlight. He pressed down a switch and light spilled out from beneath another door. He heard a stifled whimper of anticipation and smiled as he undid the latch. He entered and almost disappeared beneath a tide of foxhounds.

Asher stood no more than five feet six inches in his boots—when Archer, the big dog-hound, stood up with his forepaws on the huntsman's shoulders, they looked each other straight in the eye.

"Archer," he said, "Archer. Now, old dog—"

He pushed the big hound down and started to move through the mêlée of pressed bodies, addressing each hound by name, bending to look at torn ears and tender pads, talking in the same soft, hypnotic voice:

"Manager, Manager, here boy, Manager...Lictor, good feller, Lictor...here, Workman, Workman, here Workman, let's have a look ... Tyrant, Tyrant old dog, here then ..."

And the hounds pressed round him, trying to catch his eye, tails waving with pleasure when they did. As soon as each hound had been spoken to and touched, it turned away and climbed up on to the benches, until at last they all sat or lay in the deep litter of straw, watching him and yawning, ready now to settle down for the night. After a last look round he left them and went through to the house.

An hour later he was sitting in his dressing-gown in front of the fire. He had bathed and eaten a light meal and now he wanted nothing more than to be able to doze without interruption for an hour or so, before going to bed.

His wife came in and put a mug of tea on the table beside him, then sat down in the easy chair on the other side of the fire. She was almost Asher's height, but had a different build entirely; where he was thin and wiry, she was stocky, yet not muscular—her body was soft and comfortable. Her short brown hair was naturally curly, and already flecked with gray. After twenty-six years with Asher, she still loved him deeply—although she would never have dreamed of telling him so. An outburst of emotion from either one of them would have embarrassed and confused the other. Thus they lived, and expressed their love for each other in their own way; in forbearance and patience and an unquestioning acceptance of their union.

She looked at him now, as he stared into the fire—looked lovingly at his gypsy's profile, his high cheek-bones and deep-set eyes. She never knew what he was thinking about, but often found her own way to the answer.

"Glad it's over?" she ventured.

"Hm?"

She had expected that, and was ready to repeat the question, without impatience:

"Are you glad the season's over?"

He gave no sign that he had heard, but she knew that he had, and that he was thinking about it, and knew also that he would answer when he had thought.

"Aye, I s'pose I am," he said, at last. "It's not as easy as it used to be."

"How's your back tonight?"

"Not too bad, love."

There was a comfortable silence for a while, during which he finished his tea and put the empty mug on the floor beside him.

"How was Mr. Kendrick?" Cathie asked, after a while.

"All right," he replied. "It's not been a bad season, you know."

"I'm glad," she said, and then quietly: "I often think of him sitting up there in that big house, all on his own. He must get terrible lonely sometimes, without her."

He nodded, silently.

"They were so close," she said, gazing into the fire—both of them looking into the flames and seeing the same picture in their minds; Kendrick sitting in his study in the middle of the great empty house—sitting alone and upright in his old armchair, like half a person.

"Asher?"

From the hesitant quality in her voice, he knew what was coming.

"Did you talk to him about retiring?"

"No Cathie, I didn't. I've told you: as long as he goes on, I will, too—and that's final." He saw the disappointment in her face and went on: "Come on, gal, it's not as bad as that. I just get a bit stiff sometimes, that's all."

"Asher, you're not a young man any more."

He smiled wryly.

"You don't have to tell me, love."

They heard the distant booming of the iron door-knocker. As Cathie got up to answer it, Asher frowned: he was comfortable and unwilling to change his mood for some chance caller. Before she came back into the room Cathie was calling out: "It's all right, it's only Tod."

Asher settled back; he looked up as the old greenskeeper came in and motioned him to Cathie's chair. (It was understood that she would leave them to talk. She always did.) But instead of sitting down immediately, as he usually did—the old man stood over him, fumbling in one of the deep pockets of his overcoat, and muttering; then his face cleared. "Ah," he said. He pulled something out and placed it gently into Asher's lap, then sat down and waited for a reaction.

It was a fox-cub—little more than a week old and only six or seven inches long. Its eyes were open, but still had the blue translucence of infancy. Its short fur was damp and bedraggled and it was shivering. Asher saw a dark stain round its head and parted the fur with gentle fingers: there was a gash above the cub's left eye that stretched almost to the ear.

"Poor little devil," he said. "Who did this, d'you reckon?"

"I dunno," the old man growled morosely, "but I'd like to get me hands on 'em—"

"Did you find the others?"

Tod shook his head, staring into the fire. Asher looked down at the cub in his lap.

"They'll be dead, anyway," he murmured, more to himself than anyone.

The cub, which had been lying motionless but for its trembling, was now trying to crawl inside Asher's dressing-gown. He helped it in a little way and covered it with the warm material. Inside his clothes he could feel the tiny paws still working, working, as the cub tried to burrow in, towards the warmth of his body.

"It's dying," he said.

The old man shook his head fiercely. "It ain't dead yet," he said.

"Well..." Asher amended. "It will be soon, at any rate—I may as well knock it on the head, poor little beast."

"Leave it be," Tod muttered, so low that Asher barely heard.

Cathie came in with a mug of home-made soup for Tod, which he accepted with wordless gratitude and drank noisily, holding it in both his big, gnarled hands. While he supped, Asher opened the front of his dressing-gown and peered in at the fox-cub; it had stopped burrowing and now lay still; its trembling, too, had almost ceased. He reached in and lifted the cub out, then held it up and looked at it closely. It was limp and its eyes were almost closed.

"I'd better put it out of its misery," he murmured—then he remembered something:

"I know," he said, "I'll put it in with old Ruin—she only gave birth last week. If she takes to it, it might survive, and if she doesn't then it won't be there in the morning. At least it'll have a chance."

He was already moving towards the door that led to the kennels. When he had gone, the old man let himself quietly out of the house and disappeared into the night.

Asher made his way through the building to the paddock where the female hounds were sleeping. He located Ruin's wooden kennel and leaned over the bottom door, holding the cub carefully in both hands. He heard the soft *thump, thump* as her tail beat the ground with pleasure, and knew that she would not get up to greet him for fear of disturbing her five young pups. He opened the door quietly and knelt down in front of her.

"Ruin," he murmured, "Ruin, Ruin. There, old girl—" Gently he set the cub down with its nose towards her belly, while fonding her head with his free hand. Then, still talking to her, he stood up and backed out, closing the door behind him. He had meant to wait for a while before going, but instead he hurried away. The experiment might fail, and if so he didn't want to be there.

Asher was awake. Although his breathing was slow and even, Cathie knew by some quality in his stillness that he was awake. She turned towards him and saw a faint glimmer reflected from his eye as he lay staring up at the ceiling.

"What is it, Asher?" she whispered.

"Nothing," he replied—then, after a long pause: "It's that cub."

"Are you worried about it?"

"Aye."

She lay beside him, looking at his profile; the nose, like the prow of a ship, limned in moonlight against the darkness; the straight upper-lip and the firm mouth; the chin that jutted forward obstinately...

"Try to sleep," she whispered.

He woke as the stars began to pale, just before dawn. He dressed, groping for his clothes in the darkness, not switching on the light for fear of disturbing Cathie. As he crept from the room he heard her murmur in her sleep, like a child.

The kennels were deep in a breathing silence but he knew that heads were lifting and pointing, with ears cocked and nostrils questing towards his quiet footsteps. He felt his hounds' sudden attention as a physical sensation.

In the paddock behind the kennels the silence had a different texture—it was rich with the movement of grass and trees in the gentle dawn wind. Asher felt the air moving against his cheek, cold and damp yet not unpleasant. His feet left a dark track as he walked across the dew-soaked grass, and the roofs of the puppy-kennels gleamed wet against the distant mass of Kennel Wood.

When he looked over the half-door into Ruin's kennel nothing moved. The old female lay in a deep sleep with her young clustered against her chest and belly.

Asher counted them, and felt a sharp pang of disappointment when he made only five heads. He lingered for a moment and was about to walk away when a movement arrested him. He peered hard into the shadow beneath the dog's leg and saw the tiny, dark-furred body of the fox-cub, huddled between her hind-legs for warmth. "Good old Ruin," he said, and at the sound of his voice Ruin woke with a start; she relaxed as she identified him and started licking the puppy nearest her head.

Asher walked back to the house, aware of a need to share the secret. He went quietly up the stairs and into the small room where his daughter slept. He stood over the bed looking down at her; she was lying on her side with her brown hair tumbled over the pillow and partly over her face; her left hand was lying just in front of her mouth, the fingers half-curled. This sense of disbelief and wonder was something that had never faded since the first time he looked down at her, fourteen years before. She had been born after twelve years of marriage, long after they had given up all hope for ever having a child.

Asher reached down and lifted a strand of hair

from her cheek. He put his forefinger into the girl's half-closed fist and moved it gently.

"Jenny," he said. "Jenny, wake up."

He lifted her from the warm cocoon of her bed, wrapped a rug around her and carried her carefully down the stairs and out of the house. She was still drowsy, like a dormouse waking in spring, and at first she put her arms round his neck and her face into his shoulder, but the cold air roused her and she lifted her head and looked around.

"Where are we going?" she asked.

His nostrils caught the toothpaste-and-sleep fragrance of her breath and he felt a constriction in his chest, like a hand clenching.

"I've got a surprise for you," he said.

"Oh! where?"

She came alive in his arms, and struggled to see his face so that she could judge the truth of what he was saying. He turned his head and looked into her eyes; he saw the distant woods and the sky reflected there, then pulled back the focus of his vision so that he could see the eyes themselves; wide and intent and a little crossed with the nearness of their heads, the light golden-brown of the irises glowing in the clear light.

"Wait and see," he said.

The track that his feet had made in the dew showed faintly—Jenny saw it and looked ahead to where it led.

"Ruin?" she said.

Asher looked mysterious and said nothing; she pummelled his shoulder with her fists in exasperation. They reached the kennel and he undid the latch and opened the half-door. Jenny wriggled out of his arms and stood on the threshold, looking down at Ruin. The pups were all suckling, pushing and pawing in the eagerness of their morning hunger, oblivious to the watchers. Jenny turned and looked up at Asher, a puzzled frown on her face.

"Look again," he said.

She turned back and looked again—saw the pushing domed heads of the puppies in a row, then something else, something darker . . . she knelt so as to see more clearly, and froze in wonder as the fox-cub turned its head and looked straight at her . . . She saw its eyes, deep brown with the faint bloom that lingers for a while after they first open; she saw the soft fuzz, licked clean by Ruin during the night; the button nose, more like a toy's than an animal's; the rounded torn ears, one of them by a jagged line which reached down almost to the corner of the eye; a dribble of milk running down from the corner of the mouth and losing itself in the soft fur between the front legs . . . all this she saw in one long moment of wonder. Holding her breath she stretched out her hand towards the cub; it watched her steadily until she was almost touching it, then exploded in a hiccup of infantile fury; she felt the needle-touch of its teeth and jerked her hand back, startled by the unexpected attack. She looked up at her father, half smiling and half ashamed at being routed by such a ridiculous little creature.

"He's a proper tiger," Asher said.

She nodded and looked back at the cub; it was sitting uncertainly on its tail, looking at her. As she made no further move, it appeared to lose interest; crawling over the nearest pup. Asher tensed as Ruin lifted her head and stretched across to sniff at the interloper, but to his relief she merely licked it a couple of times before returning her head to its cushion of straw.

"Come on," Asher said, "let's leave them to get to know each other."

When he went to pick her up again she said; "No, Daddy, I want to walk on the grass."

"All right, love," he said, and draped the rug

across her shoulders; she wrapped it around her and they started back towards the kennels, hand in hand.

"Where did it come from?" she asked.

"Tod brought it, last night."

"What's happened to its mother?"

"Somebody knocked her off, I suppose."

"Why?"

"Some people don't like foxes."

She fell silent, as though digesting this information, and was still quiet when they entered the kennels. As they crossed the feeding-yard, Asher heard somebody moving about in the valeting-room. He went over to the half-open door and called: "Frank?"

The lined face of the kennelman appeared round the door:

"Morning, chief," he said—then seeing Jenny; "Morning, missy."

"Frank, keep away from Ruin's kennel, will you? And when Stephen gets in, tell him, too."

"Oh, aye. Nothing wrong with the old girl, is there?"

"No she's all right," Asher called back as he walked on towards the house, "but there's a fox-cub in with her and I want them left alone for a bit."

He was already out of the feeding-yard and halfway down the passage towards the house, so he missed Frank's reaction—he started off; "Right, chief, I'll—" then he stopped dead and his eyes opened a little wider..."a *fox*-cub?"

When they entered the warmth of the kitchen, Cathie was already at the stove, wrapped in a shapeless dressing-gown. Before Asher had shut the door behind him she had pushed Jenny into a chair and was rubbing her feet briskly with a towel, scolding them both as she did so.

"I don't know what he thinks he's doing," she was

saying, "dragging you out into the cold air with next-to-nothing on and then letting you stand in that grass in your bare feet—he ought to know better—" Jenny was taking it calmly; she knew that she had to bear the brunt of it, for Cathie would never dare scold Asher directly. As a result, Jenny caught it all, but without rancor—for Cathie never could completely hide the warmth behind her anger, and her love and concern always showed through. Satisfied at last that pneumonia had been averted—if only for the moment—Cathie stood up and told Jenny to go upstairs and get dressed. As she turned towards the stove, she heard the back door close quietly, and knew that Asher had gone out to begin the day's routine in the kennels. She started to prepare the breakfast, her hands performing automatically their ritual movements over bread-board and frying-pan and kettle. Her resentment struggled for a while, and then sank in the growing preoccupation of bringing breakfast up to yet another pitch of daily perfection. She cracked five eggs into the big iron frying-pan, then wiped her face on the sleeve of her dressing-gown and breathed in deeply.

This was the shape of her life. This was what their life together had grown into. It was all there was.

Chapter Three

HUNT KENNELS ARE not the ideal place to spend the winter, especially if you like comfort and leisure. Discipline is rigorous and the work arduous for both man and beast. Consequently, when the season comes to an end, everyone feels the need to unwind a little—even the hounds. Or, perhaps, especially the hounds. For six months or more they have been kept at a peak of fitness to enable them to cover anything up to sixty or seventy miles in the space of a few hours, and that twice or three times a week. It's a tough business—no wonder a foxhound's hunting career seldom exceeds five years.

So, with the end of the season, life became a little easier for everyone, and each day was very much the same as the one before: a routine of cleaning, feeding and walking out the hounds. Only the work of skinning and breaking up carcasses for the two great boilers remained a difficult and unpleasant job, which could not be avoided.

At the back of the kennels, in the paddock, the female hounds were bringing up their families. Some of them had given birth in February and their puppies were already six weeks old, boisterous and demanding. For these dogs the kennel staff had provided wire-netting enclosures about two and a half feet high—low enough to allow the harassed mother to escape her tumultous family for long spells. In a month's time, or even less, they would have lost all interest in their progeny and the weaning process would be complete.

These were the "Early puppies," the other dogs, some of whom had given birth only a week previously, were still shut in with their litters, and these were known as "Late puppies." Ruin had been the last to give birth, and it was to be her last litter. She was one of Asher's favorites, partly because of her qualities while hunting and partly because she had given him some good young hounds. Now, however, she was seven years old, and Asher had hesitated for a long time before finally letting her give birth to a final litter. The reason for his doubt was that aging mothers tend to have smaller progeny, and Asher liked to keep the pack up to a good standard size. In the end the temptation was too great—he wanted to try to produce a really good hound litter.

Looking over her litter when they were ten days old, and just opening their eyes, Asher was disappointed. They were sturdy enough, and their coloring was good, but they were definitely on the small side. It seemed the experiment had failed.

"Never mind, old Ruin. Never mind, old girl," he murmured, and she thrust her head against his hand and thrashed her tail in a paroxysm of adoration. He reached out and fondled one of the pups—it squirmed evasively. Acting on impulse, Asher stretched his hand towards the fox-cub, which sat huddled in the corner. Long before the hand arrived it opened its mouth in a baby snarl, pink tongue curled between hardly-visible teeth. Disturbed by the cub's distress, Ruin went to it and licked it vigorously and reassuringly—so much so, indeed, that the cub was knocked over backwards; it struggled to regain its feet and its defensive posture while the mother continued to lick it resoundingly on its belly and face. While it was still struggling ineffectually, Asher left.

*   *   *

Kendrick stepped out into the sharp morning air. He breathed deeply a couple of times, filling his lungs with the subtle smells of early April, then set off across the gardens. Halfway up the hill, towards the long, low shape of the kennels, he stopped and turned to look back at the house: so solid, so... *right*, somehow, in its context of lawns and trees. And he knew every stone of it—every slate, every leaded pane, every wooden block... knew it and loved it with an intensity that bordered on obsession. He shook his head, almost imperceptibly... *I'm fifty-five*, he thought. *Eight years ago I was... forty-seven. On my forty-seventh birthday I'd only been inside that house half a dozen times in my whole life—and now*... he shook his head again—*eight years... is that all it's been?* He turned and walked slowly on up the hill.

The sound of a door closing jerked him out of his reverie; he looked up and saw that he was almost at the kennels and Asher had just emerged to meet him.

"Morning, Mr. Kendrick," the huntsman called.

"Morning, Ash."

"Are you ready, sir?"

"Fire away."

Asher turned and shouted:

"Right, Stephen—let 'em come."

Moments later a flood of foxhounds swept out through the doorway and surged round Asher, almost hiding the small, slim figure in a tide of tan, black and white. As he moved forward, Kendrick pushed his way carefully through the pressed bodies and fell in beside Asher. The huntsman was chirruping to his hounds as he went, calling their names, as he saw them, in his soft voice: "Hazard, Hazard... Actress, there old girl, Actress... Valiant, here old dog... Reveller, Reveller... Careless, Careless then..." and the hounds, as always so full of life and movement yet listening, listening for that quiet voice to call to them, packing closely around him as they moved forward and down the hill away from the kennels.

If Asher's position was central, Stephen's was peripheral; he roved behind the pack and to each side, sending strays back to the fold with a flick of his whip or a muttered, "Have a care, sir—get on back to 'im," for Asher would not tolerate loud rating,* except in extreme circumstances. When exercising hounds this was the principal job of the whipper-in; to keep the pack together in a bunch around the huntsman, and to correct any display of bad manners. With Asher it was not too difficult a task, for the hounds loved the little man and would always fly to his voice whenever he wanted them together.

As he walked in the middle of his hounds, Asher was looking them over, judging their condition after the physical demands of the season's hunting; looking for prominent backbones and ribs, for dull, bristling coats or a listless manner. All the time his mind was storing information for later action; he saw that Furrier was going short on his off-fore, that Rapture's ear was still troubling her, that Comrade was picking his way carefully over stony ground to ease his sore pads, and so on. All in all, he thought, their condition wasn't too bad, after a long, hard winter.

They reached the bottom of the hill and followed the bridle-path into Kennel Wood. The early sharpness was wearing off rapidly; the woods around them were bursting with life, and the day was becoming mellow. Kendrick cast his eye over the gleaming coats of the hounds and felt the familiar surge of pride that they should be *his*. They

---

* To 'rate' a hound: to scold it, to speak angrily to it.

were a good pack of hounds—and not only good, but famous for their quality; the Belstone blood, which ran in the veins of hounds in almost every pack in the country. When he thought about it, he felt the beginnings of a warm glow at the center of him.

"They're beautiful, aren't they?" he murmured, not realizing that he was voicing his thoughts.

Asher nodded.

"Aye, not too bad."

Kendrick turned and looked at him sharply—then he relaxed and walked on again, smiling inwardly at his own readiness to sense antagonism. After eight years as Master, Kendrick was still aware of a deep-lying sense of insecurity. Perhaps because he came of a working-class family and had made his own way to where he now stood, he could never calmly accept his position of authority. Trying to compensate for his own unsureness, he often appeared brusque and unsympathetic in the hunting field; while he had fooled some of the people for much of the time, Asher had seen through it from the start. During the difficult period after the death of Lord Belstone, when opinions had been divided over the merits, or otherwise, of the old man's successor, Asher had been quick to sense Kendrick's basic qualities of warmth and honesty, and the huntsman's open approval had played a large part in swinging the weight of opinion behind the new Master. Over the years, the relationship between the two men had become one of absolute mutual trust and respect—yet even now, at times, Asher's natural taciturnity and economy of speech would catch him on the hop.

"Isn't it marvellous..." Kendrick muttered, still smiling.

"Eh?" Asher asked, surprised.

"Oh, nothing. Just thinking—"

At that moment a high-pitched yelp distracted their attention: they turned in time to see Radiant plunge into the body of the pack, her tail well down between her legs, her rump smarting from the lash of Stephen's whip. Asher looked inquiringly at the young man.

"Riot," Stephen said. Asher nodded: it was only to be expected with the woods teeming with wild life of all sorts, and that kind of thing was best nipped in the bud. As they went on, Kendrick asked quietly, "How's he shaping, Ash?"

"Young Stephen? Not badly at all. He's a good lad and he's not afraid of work. If he has a fault, it's over-enthusiasm, and that's not a bad one."

"It's a common fault in the young," Kendrick said, "I think I might have been a bit that way meself."

"I'll believe that," Asher said, and the two men smiled, remembering other days, between two wars.

They passed the first of the three summerhouses, a graceful little building in a simple classical style that looked out over what had once been rolling parkland and was now potatoes. An inscription over the portico read: "Alicia Mary Somerville—in loving memory." And underneath it, the date: 1856.

I'd better do it now, Asher was thinking. I ought to tell him, really. I can't go on keeping it . . .

"Er . . . Mr. Kendrick, sir?"

"Mm-m?"

"Ruin's nursing a fox-cub."

"I *beg* your pardon?"

Kendrick stopped in his tracks and turned to face Asher, his face blank.

"Ruin, sir. She's nursing a fox-cub."

"Are you being serious, Ash?"

"Yes. Tod brought me a fox-cub last week. It was near dead so I put it in with old Ruin—I thought she'd eat it, as a matter of fact, but she's fostering it instead."

Kendrick stared at him for long moments, then exploded into a bellow of delight:

"Well I'll be!" he roared to the astonished hounds, "What an amazing huntsman I've got—In fact, bloody unique, I'd say!"

Out of the corner of his eye, Asher saw Stephen grinning, and shot him a murderous look, then hurried after Kendrick, who was walking on again, still declaiming:

"What a splendid arrangement—What an absolutely marvellous arrangement—Ha!"

"You don't object then?" Asher managed to get in.

"Object?" Kendrick said, still chuckling. "'Course I don't object, man. Good luck to it!"

"Thank you, sir," Asher said, much relieved.

"He's a good chap," Frank Sammells remarked in the valeting-room that evening.

"Who—Kendrick?" Stephen asked.

"Aye. I don't care what anybody says, his heart's in the right place."

Stephen stood up and started to unbutton his brown kennel-coat.

"His heart may be in the right place..." he muttered.

Frank stopped what he was doing and looked up sharply.

"But what?" he said.

Stephen pulled the kennel-coat off and turned to hang it up on one of the row of hooks on the wall.

"Well... he's not exactly a gentleman, is he?"

"Neither are you!" Frank snapped.

Stephen turned and was startled to see the anger in the little man's face.

"I know that," he said, "but then I don't pretend I am, do I?"

"Neither does he."

"Look, what are you getting worked up about,

Frank? I just made an ordinary remark, and you—"

"You're always making remarks about Mr. Kendrick and I don't like it."

"All right, all right," Stephen soothed, "I'm sorry—I didn't mean any harm."

The kennelman went back to greasing the thong of a hunting-whip, and said nothing. Stephen looked at him for a moment, then shrugged and took his jacket from its peg.

"For a peaceful little man," he remarked equably, "you don't half go at me sometimes."

Frank tired to keep his face straight, but it was impossible—he grinned sheepishly, as Stephen had known he would, and put the whip down on the table.

"I don't think you're fair to him," he said, "that's what gets me."

Stephen shrugged.

"Maybe . . ." he said, struggling into his jacket.

"Just because he's made his own money and doesn't talk like a . . . well, because he talks a bit like I do—that doesn't mean he isn't a good chap. I tell you what; I reckon the Hunt would have folded up when his Lordship died if it hadn't been for him."

"And his money," Stephen remarked.

"There you go again!" Frank almost shouted: "You can't leave him alone, can you?"

"Sorry, sorry," Stephen said, hurriedly, "I don't mean these things the way you think I do, honestly."

But this time the old kennelman was not to be mollified; he picked up the whip and started rubbing grease energetically, puffing over his work like an old-fashioned groom. After a moment Stephen turned away and crossed the room to the door.

"'Night, Frank," he said, as he opened the door.

"'Night," the kennelman growled, without looking up. Stephen smiled and closed the door gently behind him.

Leaving the kennels by the back entrance he almost bumped into Jenny. She was out of breath from running and her cheeks were glowing. Stephen grabbed her by the arm as she passed and swung her round to face him.

"Hey!" he said, "what's the hurry?"

"Let me go!" she demanded, laughing.

"Not until you've told me what's the hurry."

"You're a bully, Stephen Durno."

Stephen grinned and held on—she was so bursting-full of life that it would have been impossible not to be affected by it.

"Come on," he insisted, "I want to know."

Suddenly she twisted away from him, broke his grip on her arm and ran, laughing back at him over her shoulder. He went to run after her, but she had disappeared into the kennels before he got properly started, so he gave up and continued on his way home. Within minutes he was thinking about something else and did not recall the incident once during the rest of the evening. Yet in bed that night, lying between wakefulness and sleep he remembered Jenny: her sparkling gray eyes, her dark hair flying... soon after that, he slept.

It was while Jenny was trying to think up a name for the fox-cub that Cathie first described Ruin's mixed litter as the "Rag, Tag and Bobtail Brigade." Jenny pounced on this with delight and chose the name "Tag" for the little creature. Asher tried hard to make her choose a better-sounding name; and indeed, she did try, looking carefully through Beckford's official list of hound-names, but she found nothing that suited her and after a couple of days Tag had stuck.

Chapter Four

CONSCIOUSNESS BEGAN DIMLY for Tag in the warmth of an enveloping darkness. Even after ten days, when his eyes opened for the first time, the darkness was unrelieved by any glimmer of light, for the mother had her litter in a deep earth. He was just becoming aware of the presence of his brothers and sisters when the terrier came. The shrill, savage yapping, only feet away from him, set his baby fur bristling and he snarled soundlessly in the darkness—a darkness which was rent suddenly as the hound's paws tore the earth apart. A blow from one of these paws broke the vixen's back as she turned at bay, blinded in the brilliant beam from a torch, and the terrier worried the rest of the life out of her with its teeth at her throat. The cubs—five of them—were picked up roughly and their heads were knocked hard against the smooth bole of the tree that stood over the violated earth. One of them was killed instantly, while three more died during the long night, but one survived ... hardly conscious, his head matted with blood from a gash through which gleamed the whiteness of bone; lying where he had been flung, motionless except for an occasional twitching and stirring of his limbs; clinging precariously to the little thread that was all that remained of his life-force—Tag lay, waiting for an old man to walk home through the woods.

* * *

Close as he was to death while Tod carried him to
the kennels and gave him to Asher, there was a
moment of even greater danger after the huntsman
put him in with Ruin's litter, and retired; the old
mother sensed the presence of something alien and
turned to investigate—at the unmistakable fox-
scent, mingled with the smell of blood, her hackles
rose and she growled deep in her throat, her canine
teeth gleaming in the moonlight. Too weakened to
be aware of his danger, Tag instinctively burrowed
into the warmth of the mother's belly. This accident
saved his life, for the blood-fury died down in her
brain and she began to lick him clean.

It was fortunate for Tag that he was almost a
week older than Ruin's puppies, for they were still
blind and weak when he arrived. But for this he
might still not have survived, for in his weakened
state he could not possibly have competed for food;
as it was, the puppies' early helplessness gave him a
respite, and by the time their eyes began to open, on
the tenth day, Tag had regained much of his
strength. As the puppies' vision cleared and they
began to investigate the world around them, the
fox-cub was already a part of that world, and as
such they accepted him from the start.

As far as Ruin was concerned, Tag was one of her
puppies. Although his chocolate-brown fur con-
trasted strongly with the tan-and-white of the pups'
shorter coats, it made no difference to the old
mother dog. The important thing, to her, was that
he smelled and tasted the same as the others—or
almost so; occasionally, when Tag was frightened
suddenly, or became excited, she would catch a
sudden whiff of fox . . . but by this time her reaction
to it had dulled to the point of non-existence, and
Tag was safe.

His wound healed; the flesh knitted and hair

began to grow again, but no longer brown; instead, a zig-zag of white began to show, like a spark jumping from the corner of his left eye to the base of his ear.

During these early days, a fox-cub exhibits few of the typical features of an adult fox. Tag had a fat body, covered in woolly fur, with stumpy legs and short tail; his head was rounded, with a blunt muzzle, small low-set ears and button eyes. The fox-hound pups looked more like the finished article, and even at two weeks they wore a worried, wrinkled expression that sat comically on their baby features.

The weather turned suddenly mild halfway through April, and the pups began to spend more and more time outside the kennel—but not Tag. He stayed behind in the shadows, worried and fretful until they returned. Somewhere deep inside his brain a clock was running—a clock which governed his development to such an extent that he was physically unable to leave the darkness of his kennel until he was a month old ... the age at which wild fox-cubs emerge from the earth and see the world around them for the first time. A week later he made his first tentative appearance outside the kennel; after ten seconds he panicked and whisked back into the friendly darkness. But it was a beginning.

The same time-sense had other effects as well; he would wake early in the morning, before dawn, and move around fitfully until the sun came up, when he would rejoin the sleeping puppies. Later, when they awoke and started to play, he would sleep on far into the day. At dusk, too, when the puppies were yawning hugely and settling down to sleep, the fox-club came to life and tried to play with them—they would have none of it, and warned him off with petulant growls. Although as time went on, Tag's habits changed slowly to adapt to those of the puppies, he never became completely diurnal—always he was up before them and after them, and always he slept more in the daytime.

During these first few weeks, Tag gradually became accustomed to the proximity of people, for Asher was a regular visitor, while Jenny spent much of her time trying to win his confidence. Fox-cubs are not born with an instinctive fear of human beings, but the murder of his family had left Tag with a strong mental association between the smell of people and the smell of death. For this reason, it was some time before he could completely accept the nearness of a human being. It was Jenny who first broke down the barrier of his fear. Although much of her character was her mother's she had inherited from Asher a way with animals. She understood the cause of Tag's fear—although she could never have expressed it in words—and divined the way to overcome it. In the mornings, before school, and during the quiet evenings, just before dark, she became another of Ruin's puppies—lying on the straw just inside the spacious kennel and doing puppyish things, falling in with the prevailing mood. Never once did she make an advance of any sort towards Tag—as long as he regarded her with suspicion, she simply pretended that he didn't even exist and got on with whatever she was doing. At feeding-time she snuggled up with her face to Ruin's belly—earning some anxious glances at first from the puzzled old dog. At playtime she roistered with the pups, and at sleepy-time she slept, not even pretending but actually falling asleep. And all the time, Tag's button eyes would follow her every move with unflagging suspicion... But he couldn't keep it up forever, of course, as Jenny well knew. Gradually her human smell began to form new associations in his baby-mind; it began to be accompanied by such reassuring images as the taste of milk, and the warmth and safety of the kennel, and at last the fox-cub relaxed his vigilance. From then on he treated Jenny as a foster-sister, and was soon crawling all over her, exploring her personal topography with a fox's characteristic blend of curiosity and imperti-nence. When Asher saw what she had done, he felt a deep glow of pride, knowing that it was one of *his* gifts to her that she was developing—and it is always a heart-warming thing to see one's gifts used, lovingly and to good effect, long after the giving.

Almost as soon as they can get around, young animals begin to play—and no one knows for certain why. There are plenty of theories; that play gets rid of excess energy; that it is a rehearsal for actions which will be useful later in life; that it establishes the social dominance, or peck-order in the family, and so on. Perhaps the truth is a blend of all these theories, and perhaps there is yet another reason, for it is hard to watch fox or otter cubs at play without feeling that there is an element of sheer exuberance and joie-de-vivre in their tumbling and capering.

While Ruin's puppies were only two or three weeks old, play consisted of lazy tussles, but as they grew and became stronger, the fighting became more vigorous, and sharp little teeth began to puncture tender skin. Although fully able to hold his own at first, Tag began to come off rather badly in these family wrangles. The pups were growing fast, and were now almost double his weight. In the beginning, his advanced development had balanced the odds, but now the puppies' superior strength was beginning to tell. Tag slid inevitably down the peck-order until he was in the bottom position. This meant that all the puppies could bite him with little fear of retaliation, and this they did, hour after hour and day after day, until Tag's life became a misery.

At this point his spirit could have broken and he

could have become an abject, cringing thing,
fawning before his superiors. But two factors
prevented this. First, he was still a wild creature and
a savage flame burned somewhere deep in his heart.
Secondly, he found support from an unexpected
quarter.

His new-found ally was the last born of Ruin's
puppies. Small and weak to begin with, he was
forced into last place in the dinner-queue and so
developed less quickly than his more robust
brothers and sisters. Had Tag not arrived, he would
inevitably have been bottom in the pecking-
order,—as it was, he occupied the place just above
the fox-cub and used his position to bully his sole
inferior whenever he could. But the passage of
another week or so altered the picture; the stronger
puppies grew bigger and stronger still, while the
youngest one developed less quickly. As their play
became increasingly rough and aggressive, both Tag
and this particular puppy came in for more and
more punishment, and in the end a curious situation
developed; the two smallest members of the family,
although widely separated by race, found themselves fighting side-by-side or back-to-back against
the rest of the world. As time went by, this accident
became something more like an arrangement; at the
first sign of a rumble, the two allies would fly to each
other, ready for whatever might come. With
practice they began to develop techniques of
retaliation, and after a brief period of serious and
sometimes bloody fighting, an even stranger
phenomenon occurred. The social dominance order
in a family once established, tends to remain
unchanged until the family breaks up. But in Ruin's
litter a *coup d'état* took place; after a pitched
battle, the single fighting unit consisting of the
puppy and the fox-cub beat the A-puppy, and took
over his place at the top of the order, relegating him
to the B position. For a little while the two

comrades-in-arms went about in a perpetual bristle and snarl, ready for the next attack to come; but the unwritten law of social dominance held firm, and no attack came. Gradually they relaxed their vigilance and began to accustom themselves to a life of new security and ease. The atmosphere in the kennel improved perceptibly and playful romping took the place once again of bad-tempered aggression.

By this time Tag was six weeks old and changing rapidly. The dark brown of his coat had given way to a beautiful golden red; the shape of his head had altered radically; his ears were larger and more pointed, and set higher on the head; his muzzle had become finer and sharper, while his eyes had lost the 'button' look of infancy; his tail was longer and a little bushier, and his legs were longer, too. No longer was he a sprawling, helpless baby; he was beginning to show the first faint promise of the elegance and grace of an adult fox. The puppies, too, were beginning to grow up; their legs seemed to be growing twice as fast as the rest of their bodies; they were beginning to explore the outside world—outside their paddock, that is. They met no opposition from old Ruin, who was content to let them go where they pleased. Already she was beginning to lose interest in them, although she mothered them whenever they could catch her. On wet days the puppies stayed mostly in the kennel and made her life a misery with their inexhaustible energy and sharp teeth. Even Tag would join in when Ruin was being bated, dashing in to the attack and whisking away out of reach before she could catch him. Sometimes it became too much for her and she would run for her life, pursued by the whole tumbling, yapping pack. Yet, for all this, she was a devoted mother to them. Most of the females loved to show off their litters and would welcome visitors with wagging tails and panting smiles, but not Ruin—only Asher and his daughter dared visit

Ruin in her kennel. If anyone else got within thirty yards she would warn them with a rumbling snarl, her hackles up and her head lowered. Any theorist who believed that her bluff could be called and approached to within ten feet or so was attacked, swiftly and decisively. Once or twice she had even snarled at Asher, and each time the huntsman had withdrawn, knowing discretion—with old foxhound females—to be the better part of valor.

May came in, soft and promising. Life was easy for the hounds as they rested and recuperated. The hunters' summer coats had grown and they were all turned out to grass. When hounds were walked past their field they would watch with ears pricked until they were out of sight, then return to their grazing. The puppies grew and frolicked and fought and grew, and Tag with them; longer and slimmer and a deeper red, a little quicker and more foxy every day.

The fox-cub's alliance with the puppy had developed into something deeper than a mutual defense agreement; they had become constant companions. While the rest of the family played amongst themselves, the two comrades played with each other, and would allow no intrusion, turning in combined fury on anyone who might try it on. Even Tag's ally was growing by this time; his new social position ensured him as much food as he could eat, and although he remained smaller than the rest of the litter he was growing stronger all the time. He and the fox-cub played with an absorbed intensity for hour after hour, and this was to his benefit, too, for Tag's speed and agility forced him to excel himself in order to be a match for the young fox. At the same time Tag was learning something from the puppy; it is a fox's nature to dash in, chop, and whisk away again—but this would not always work with his companion, and gradually Tag developed a foxhound characteristic; the quality of persistence. At sunset and sunrise they would invariably be playing together while the other puppies slept. The process was not complete, however, for when Tag prowled around in the middle of the night, his friend was not with him—even though Tag tried to wake him by prodding him with his sharp nose.

It was during one of Tag's midnight prowls that he witnessed a strange phenomenon. One of Ruin's contemporaries was a female called Browser—a rare case of a name exactly fitting a character, for she was amiable and phlegmatic. Out hunting she was a good worker, steady and unimaginative, and, for all anyone knew, her private life was the same, yet ... Browser led a double life. When Tag saw her creep out of her kennel and drift like a ghost across the moonlit paddock he followed her curiously. Blissfully unaware that she was being shadowed, old Browser trotted steadily down the hill. Soon she was picking her way round the flower-beds in the gardens of the Big House, and Tag was in territory new to him. As she drew closer to the dark mass of the house, Browser's manner became increasingly furtive; sticking close to the shadow of hedges and walls she arrived at last at the back of the house. Hidden twenty yards away in the shrubbery, Tag saw her cross the tarmac yard and stop in front of one of the dustbins. After a last guilty look around, the old female stood up and placed her paws on the rim of the dustbin, then pushed with all her strength. The dustbin toppled slowly and fell with a crash; even as the lid was rolling noisily across the yard, Browser was head-and-shoulders inside the dustbin, rummaging greedily. As the lid finally clattered on to its side—making Tag flatten with fear at the clang—she emerged with the remains of a roast pheasant in her mouth and ran from the scene, her tail between her legs and shooting fearful glances back over her shoulder as lights went on in the house. Running, she passed within feet of the crouching fox-cub but noticed nothing, so perfectly did he merge into the shadows. When the back door opened and a man emerged wearing a dressing-gown and carrying a torch, Tag fled, too. Halfway back to the kennels he heard a noise in a clump of bushes—it was Browser gleaning what she could from the stolen carcass. Tag's mouth salivated as he caught a whiff of pheasant-smell but he did not dare show himself. After a while, the old female carefully buried the remains under a tree and waddled away into the darkness; as soon as she was gone Tag dug it up again but failed to find the tiniest scrap of meat anywhere. Disappointed, he licked it for a while and then lost interest and moved on. By this time Browser was well on her way towards the nearby village of Cawsdon.

During the ensuing hours of darkness she knocked over and beachcombed seventeen dustbins in the village and surrounds, traveling nearly ten miles at a steady trot in order to do it. When she crept back into her kennel and her sleeping puppies, less than an hour before daylight, Tag did not see her, for he was asleep as well. This was Browser's secret; she was the Phantom Dustbin-Robber of Cawsdon, and she had escaped detection over five years of steady pillaging, during the months from January to June, when she was at liberty around the kennels. Not even Asher had any idea that the mysterious prowler was one of his own hounds, for his dustbin had been overturned regularly, along with everybody else's. Nor were his suspicions ever roused by Browser's own idiosyncrasy; for some reason she was a very late sleeper, and was seldom up and about before ten in the morning.

During the Easter holidays, Jenny was able to spend hours every day with Tag—and being with the fox-cub, by this time, meant being with his companion as well—which suited Jenny fine. It also suited Ruin, for, once again, motherhood was losing its glamor for the old female and she was delighted to see the back of the "twins" for an hour or two.

By the end of May, Jenny was taking them for walks across the park and into Kennel Wood. Tag enjoyed these walks right from the start, but the puppy had a few misgivings at first. Once or twice, when they were about a quarter of a mile out from the kennels, his courage failed him—with a quavering howl he made a frantic run for home, with Tag frisking and capering alongside him and Jenny—breathless and almost crying with laughter—bringing up the rear.

Ruin was spending less and less time with her family and became bad-tempered with them. She no longer played with them, and they were becoming more independent each day. They were ready to be weaned, and one day early in June, Asher weaned them.

The process of finding "walks" for the puppies had been going on for some time. As soon as a foxhound puppy is weaned, around the age of ten weeks, it is sent out to live with a member of the hunt or local well-wisher who is willing to help in this way. Sometimes singly and sometimes in pairs, the puppies stay with their hosts for a little less than a year, and are then returned to the kennels. Puppy-walkers are urged to allow their young charges as much freedom as is possible—freedom to roam the countryside and develop their initiative and resourcefulness. Then, when the young hound returns to the kennels to learn how to hunt foxes, it will be a well-developed and individual character in it s own right, rather than a mere cog in a machine.

Ruin had been the last female to give birth, and consequently her puppies were the last to be sent out to walk. By this time there were few people left who were willing to take a puppy, but Asher made enquiries and before long four of the five puppies were placed, leaving only the youngest one—and, of course, his constant companion.

Asher tattooed the litter number inside the ear of each of the puppies and settled down to name them. Their sire was Martial, so—following age-old tradition—he allotted the whole litter names beginning with the letter M (and even the names were from a traditional list of hound-names). He opened the litter-book and made the following entry:—

Age	Name	Sire	Dam
1962	MENACER	Brocklesby,	RUIN, '56
	MEANWELL	MARTIAL, '55	
	MERLIN		
	MELODY		
	MERRIMENT		

At last, Tag's companion had a name—an ancient name with dual connotations; with grace, speed and courage on the one hand, and on the other, wisdom and strength. A magic name...a fateful name...Merlin.

Chapter Five

THEY HAD DRUNK a little more tea than usual, perhaps because there had been so much to discuss.

"Right then," he said, closing the litter-book with a bang, "that takes care of that." He drained his cup, then took the pot and refilled it. "So," he said, then "Whoops—I've done it again!" He got up, with some difficulty, and took the teapot over to top up Asher's cup; the fact that it was three-quarters full didn't alter a thing—he filled it up to the brim and then sat down again. Asher glanced anxiously at his drink and wondered what he ought to do about it.

"Now, where were we?" Kendrick asked. "Oh yes, I remember—how's the walk situation?"

"One left," Asher replied.

"Which one?"

"Merlin—you know, from Ruin's litter."

"The one with the foxy friend?"

"That's the one."

"No walk?"

"No walk."

"Oh..."

Kendrick seemed lost in thought, Asher took a cautious sip from his cup and waited. Suddenly Kendrick came to life:

"Beckford!" he shouted.

Ignoring Asher's startled expression, Kendrick got up and launched himself at the book-case with his usual fierce, disorientated energy.

"Beckford," he repeated and took *Thoughts on Hunting* from a shelf. "Now let me see..." he muttered, leafing through it. "Ah, here it is—listen to this, Ash: 'I am in doubt whether it might not be better to breed them up yourself, and have a kennel on purpose. You have a large orchard paled in, which would suit them exactly; and what else is wanted might easily be obtained.' There—how about that?"

He shut the book and peered at Asher over his reading glasses, his bushy eyebrows raised satirically.

"Did Beckford really say that?" Asher asked, after a moment or two.

"He did."

"Then I don't agree with him," the huntsman said, primly.

Kendrick stared for a moment, then burst out with a bellow of laughter.

"He's done it again!" he roared exultantly. "He's done it again!"

Asher looked pained.

"What d'you mean?" he asked.

Kendrick flopped back into his armchair.

"You don't agree with Beckford!" he gasped, his eyes watering. "Oh that's marvellous..."

Asher maintained a hurt silence until at last Kendrick's laughter subsided. When all was quiet again, he said:

"Beckford was a wonderful hound-man, but he was wrong there."

Kendrick chuckled and wiped his eyes behind the glasses.

"Could be," he said, "but you might *have* to take his advice if you can't find a walk for that puppy."

Asher considered the idea. For a whole pack it was ridiculous, but perhaps for just one puppy... well, it might work. It might.

"How about the fox, Ash?" Kendrick asked.

"It'll go of its own accord."

"You sure?"

"Aye—a fox'll always go back, unless you chain it, and I'll not do that."

Kendrick nodded. The two men fell silent, staring into the dying fire and occupied with their own thoughts. The wind blew a rattle of rain against the windows, but the sound went unnoticed in the comfortable warmth. After a long time, Kendrick spoke; and his voice was no longer brash and vibrant—it was suddenly hesitant, uncertain:

"How'm I doing, Ash?"

"How're you doing at what?" Asher asked, puzzled.

"You know—everything."

Asher shook his head.

"Everything; the Hunt, the house... sitting up here and playing the squire—" he turned to face Asher—"I want you to tell me if I'm getting away with it."

Asher shook his head again, honestly perplexed, staring at Kendrick as though trying to find the answer there, in his eyes. Kendrick hitched himself forward in his chair, his bulldog head thrust forward, his hands crupping and moving round a fear that was almost too deep to identify, let alone express.

"I'm trying to do a good job," he explained, his eyes closing as he groped for words: "I'm trying my hardest not to let the old chap down—" He nodded towards a portrait of the late Lord Belstone which hung to one side of the fireplace. Asher glanced at it and felt the familiar surge of love for the Old Man, even after all these years...

"It's them that worry me," Kendrick muttered: "I don't know what they're saying about me behind my back—that's what gets me..." He exploded suddenly: "Tell me what they're saying, Ash. I want to know."

"But . . . why me? Why ask me?"

Asher was perplexed and unhappy; he recognized the cause of Kendrick's outburst—but he could not find the words to allay the fear and the doubt.

"I don't know," he said, frowning: "I don't know what people say, and I wouldn't care if I did."

Kendrick had relapsed again into silence. Asher watched as the strength began to creep back into his face, which gradually lost its haunted, hunted look. After a long time Kendrick drew a deep breath, and then chuckled.

"Silly fool," he murmured, still staring into the dying fire. Asher relaxed as he saw that the crisis had passed. After a short silence, Kendrick said quietly:

"You know, Ash, you were the first person around here to accept me for what I am."

Asher could think of nothing to say, and remained silent.

"And that means a lot to me," Kendrick added.

Some days later, Asher decided to adopt Kendrick's suggestion and keep Merlin himself; it seemed the only thing to do in the circumstances. He stood at the paddock gate one evening, smoking his pipe, and watched Merlin and Tag playing near their kennel. They were alone in the field, yet completely happy in each other's company as they played some kind of game round the empty kennels. Perhaps for the first time, Asher really looked at Merlin and as he did so he began to notice things which had escaped him before; he noticed the way the young hound moved—although still at the leggy stage, he was quick and graceful. He noticed the shining coat and the look of potential speed and strength, which might in time outweigh his small size. After a long, careful look, he began to feel better about walking Merlin himself. He switched his attention to the fox-cub—at that moment stalking Merlin like a cat, his rump stuck up in the air, his tail quivering—and smiled when he thought of the bedraggled bundle that had just filled his cupped hands only two months before.

Suddenly he found himself looking at Tag— *looking*, with all his mind focussed—and began to really see the young fox for the first time. For so many years his life had been closely involved with foxes, and perhaps this is why he had never really looked—because the fox, to him, was simply Charles James; "orthodox," as they used to say. Foxes did this and never did that... always the generic noun: "foxes," or the camouflage of "Charlie"... but now here was Asher Smith, professional foxhunter, looking at *A Fox*... and a very special fox, at that, for he had saved its life. This thought came to Asher as something of a shock, and almost immediately, he understood why; it is paradoxical, but true, that if you save somebody's life, the debt of gratitude that remains goes *both ways*—so that by saving Tag from death that March night, he had incurred a sense of gratitude towards the life that he had saved. Asher turned this thought over in his mind; he knew not only that it was true, but also that he had known it for quite some time without ever actually facing it...

Asher came out of his reverie and looked around for the two young animals; he saw Merlin straight away, stretched out in the doorway of the wooden kennel, but there was no sign of Tag—then he glimpsed a flash of russet from the corner of the paddock, where the disused kennels were stored. Following an impulse, Asher put his pipe down on the ground and started walking slowly towards the empty kennels.

Tag was rooting around in his usual way, confident that his labors would be rewarded by a succulent slug or a scrap of rotting meat, when suddenly he saw Asher... The huntsman was standing quite still, no more than four or five yards away, watching him calmly. Tag was not frightened—merely puzzled; he stood for a while, frozen in mid-movement, one delicate black paw raised, motionless, apart from the twitching of his nostrils and the flicker of one ear towards a distant sound.

Asher gazed curiously at the fox-cub and felt a thrill of pleasure at his absolute grace and poise. Tag's slanted amber eyes held his gaze unflinchingly and returned it, without fear. Asher moved forward very slowly; Tag watched him approach until he was only a few feet away—then stepped one pace back, calmly and deliberately. Asher realized that this approach was not going to work, so he lowered himself carefully to his knees and then back on to his heels, to wait. Tag watched curiously as Asher gazed at him, noticing the highlights that shimmered in the silky chestnut coat; the silver-white under jaw, throat and chest; the long brush, already showing a white tip; the gazelle-like limbs, dark and slim... *What a beautiful creature,* he was thinking—*I never realized just how beautiful...* then he let go of the thought as Tag's curiosity at last overcame his reserve and he walked delicately up to Asher and stood frankly before him, investigating him with his pointed, sensitive nose. "Hallo, son," Asher murmured, almost inaudibly. Tag pricked his ears at the sound but showed no fear. Encouraged, Asher put his hand up to stroke the fox's head—for a moment Tag stiffened; his eyes narrowed and the corners of his mouth pulled back; but Asher paused and remained still, so that the momentary fear died. As soon as he saw Tag relax, he allowed his hand to continue its movement until it lay against the silky ruff that framed the fox's face. He rubbed gently with his thumb, towards the roots of the hair, and after a few moments was rewarded, when Tag turned his head and leaned into the caress.

"There, you see?" Asher said, "I didn't eat you, did I?"

Tag looked into his eyes as he spoke, and Asher noticed again how steadily and calmly the fox held his gaze—unlike most animals, who feel it as a threat. Tag's acceptance of him, in the end, came quickly and completely; with a graceful movement, the young fox placed his fore-paws on Asher's knee, stood upright and licked the huntsman delicately across his face.

It was something that had never happened to the huntsman, so its impact was unmitigated by familiarity; in a sudden rush of feeling, he recognized the ties that bound them, even then, each to the other. For a solitary moment in time a door opened in his consciousness, then closed again—but it was long enough for him to be touched by what lay beyond the door.

Chapter Six

THE TREES WERE in full, soft leaf. The late afternoon sunlight filtered through the canopy of foliage and filled the depths of the wood with a dim luminescence. Everywhere there was a whisper of hidden life and movement—invisible yet perceptible, like a pulse in the blood.

A stream flowed through the wood, moving lazily over a gravel bed with few rocks to impede its progress. In the shallows, where the stream changed its course, patches of fragrant meadowsweet swayed gently, while rich purple masses of loose-strife seemed to glow in the shadow of the banks.

The clear water was dancing with insect-life; pond-skaters and whirligig beetles made crazy patterns on the surface, while beneath the surface moved water-boatmen, water-beetles and the countless larvae of a dozen different species; the sinister shape of a water-scorpion lurked in a tangle of weed, and dragon-fly larvae stalked the stream-bed like prehistoric tigers. Above the stream, mayflies dipped and shimmered on filigree wings, dimpling the surface where they brushed it and filling the luminous dusk with dancing motes of light.

In the trees and the undergrowth all around, harassed birds were making their last visits to the nest, beaks crammed with insects and grubs for the gape-mouthed fledglings, almost as big now as their parents. In other nests lay the second clutch of eggs—the first brood having left only days before to start life on their own—and the mother-birds were already settling down to brood them for the night, shuffling their feet and rousing their feathers to achieve a perfect fit. A family of four young thrushes were arranging themselves in a row to roost for the night, fully-fledged now and supposedly independent but still sticking together for warmth and company; they shuffled and nudged one another and glared sleepily, feathers roused and eyes oval with drowsiness. At last they were comfortable and blinked for a while before putting their heads, one by one, over their shoulders and under their wings, to sleep. The whole world seemed to be blinking and shuffling its feet in the same way, as though waiting for the last horizontal beams from the setting sun to wink out, like lights in a city. The smooth boles of the great trees were dappled with gently moving pools of golden light, and the leaves that formed the forest roof were beginning to whisper with the first stirring of the night wind.

One moment that was everything, and the next moment there was Tag, too, standing motionless in a clearing, his red-gold coat like a flame in the dusk. He stood absolutely still—his only movement the twitching of nostrils as he tasted the cool air; his black-tipped ears were pricked and his eyes smouldered with an amber fire, the pupils almost round in the dim light. For long minutes he stood like this, as though bewitched at the center of a spreading stillness—then a dry twig snapped explosively in the silence, and moments later Merlin emerged from the undergrowth in a flurry of noise and movement.

The two young animals started to play along the bank of the stream—lazily at first but with a growing excitement, until at last they were whirling and leaping like demented spirits, in total abandon.

They broke off, exhausted for the moment, and lapped water from the stream, standing side by side in their own fragmented images. They finished at the same time and stood for a few moments, indecisively; then Merlin turned and licked the fox-cub a couple of times, across the side of the face. Together they clambered up the bank and trotted off into the depths of the wood with Tag leading and Merlin a few paces behind.

They slept that night in the middle of a briar-patch, on a bed of rich leaf-mould. Merlin lay stretched out on his side, with Tag curled up in the space between his fore and his hind legs. The young hound slept deeply, his limbs twitching at times as he dreamed, but Tag slept more lightly: from time to time he lifted his head to listen or to test the air, and once he stood up—carefully, so as not to disturb his companion—and lay down again, curled the other way.

An hour before dawn he was fully awake. He stood up and stretched then turned to wake Merlin. He touched his companion once with his muzzle, and when this failed he gave a high-pitched growl that ended in a yelp. Merlin woke with a start and sat up, then yawned hugely and scratched behind his ear with a hind foot. He followed obediently when Tag slipped out of the briars, still yawning, but game.

It was a time of learning, for both of them. With the richness of June all around them, the living was easy. Succulent black slugs, scurrying beetles (that tickled deliciously in the mouth before the satisfying *crunch*), earthworms, caterpillars, grubs and woodlice. The world was a treasure-house of fascinating smells, some known, some unknown, and some with hidden meanings. They lived through their noses, the two young animals, and their quick young brains were sifting and storing the information that they gained. It was a simple procedure, and one at which Tag excelled; it went rather like this: *smell...a new smell...where? ...over there...investigate...*and he locates it and sniffs at it: If it jumps and runs away, *after it like the clappers!* If it stings or bites or claws *think carefully before doing anything rash...leave it alone, perhaps.* If it just sits there and goes on smelling *try it...*a lick first, then another...then a bite. If it tastes nasty *spit it out! Yuck! And don't do that again.* And if it tastes good then that's another one for the list of eatables. Of course, Tag was no more capable of this form of reasoning than a cabbage, but—interpreted in human terms—that is how it happened; prompted by innate reflexes to investigate, Tag would then associate the object of the investigation with one of the number of emotional possibilities: hostile, or good to eat, or merely uninteresting. Thus, the next time his nostrils picked up that particular smell, the relevant association would be ready and would allow him to act accordingly and correctly. One of the reasons for this instinctive process in a young fox is that foxes are omnivorous—they will eat anything that is remotely edible, and that includes rotting food-stuffs, carrion and all sorts of trash. So, by trial and error, a young fox gradually learns what can be eaten and what should be left alone.

Merlin's approach was quite different. His tastes were far less catholic than Tag's, and he was born with an instinctive appreciation of what was going to taste nice. When hungry, he would be thrown into a violent excitement by the smell of a rabbit or a squirrel. Because of his youth and inexperience he was unable, as yet, to catch his quarry, but at least he knew its identity. Food was put down every morning at the kennels, so there was no real problem; and in the meanwhile he was learning how to use his nose to follow up the elusive creatures of the woods—after many mistakes, learning how to stick to one trail, distinguishing it from other scents that might cross it or coincide with it for a while.

So, while Tag was learning to hunt like a fox and while Merlin was learning how to hunt like a hound, something else was happening at the same time . . . because of their constant proximity, each was picking up something of the ways of the other. Merlin was beginning to learn the opportunist methods of a fox, while Tag sometimes found himself sticking to an animal's line and hunting it, like a hound.

If a hound that knows all about foxes is called a foxhound, then couldn't you call a fox that knows all about hounds a houndfox? That, at any rate, is what they were becoming as they learned from their environment and from each other; Foxhound and Houndfox.

The first time the two animals became aware of the silent figure that watched them, they were frightened and ran away . . . but after a while they came to accept him as part of the woods around them. Sometimes they were aware of his presence and at other times they were not—it depended on a number of factors such as wind direction and strength, scenting conditions, and so on. But night after night he was there; usually for an hour or so after sunset and often before dawn as well; his tall, stooping frame wrapped in a huge old overcoat. And when they were aware of him it did not disturb them, for he presented no threat. As the summer burgeoned, Tod watched the two animals, and learned.

Chapter Seven

WHEN TAG AND MERLIN started sleeping out in the woods instead of coming back to their kennel, Asher was worried; he was afraid that Tag might entice Merlin away altogether. After a while he saw that the two companions continued to return for food every day, and worried less. Sometimes, for no apparent reason, they would turn up at the kennels and stay for a while, sleeping in their old home and spending the days prowling around the buildings and making a nuisance of themselves at the flesh-hovel, where they hung around for hours, hoping for scraps.

During one of these visits, towards the end of June, Asher noticed that Tag had become very noisy in the evenings and around dawn. A few weeks earlier, their play had been accompanied only by juvenile growls and an occasional yelp of pain, but now Tag was letting go an increasing assortment of yells, yaps and screams—and other sounds, too, which are difficult to transcribe: a sort of hiccup, which seemed to indicate alarm or anger; a churring or chucking sound; and even a loud hissing, for all the world like an enraged goose. The result was comical when Merlin tried to emulate, for his larynx was a radically different structure. All he could manage was a somewhat hysterical howling and a wheezing noise, which probably hurt his throat because he quickly gave up the attempt and left it all to Tag.

In July, hound exercise began and the Hunt staff had far more work to do. The tempo in the kennels was beginning to quicken and would continue to do so until a plateau of endeavor was reached at the beginning of the hunting season. They clattered out on to the road at 6 a.m. the first morning, with the excited hounds milling around Asher's horse, a sea of waving tails. As they jogged off down the road, Tag and Merlin watched them go: two secret pairs of eyes in an overgrown ditch.

A few days later, Merlin caught his first live quarry. For some time Tag had been catching small rodents and birds, but luck had eluded Merlin, who lacked the fox's speed and opportunism. Now, however, the countryside was full of young birds who were still learning to fly, and it was one of these that got up almost from under the young hound's nose one afternoon. The fledgling—it was a blackbird—took off for cover, but lacked the strength to gain height. Merlin set off in delirious pursuit, his progress punctuated by shrill yelps of excitement. Just before the chase reached the edge of a copse, it was suddenly over, and Merlin had made his first kill. He ate the morsel of still-warm flesh, sneezing at the downy feathers that gathered round his muzzle, then trotted off to find Tag.

When Merlin had gone, Tod emerged from the cover of the woods, fifty yards downwind, and walked slowly to the little scattering of feathers. He stood looking down at them as they shivered and blew in the warm breeze, and saw the few spots of blood on the grass. He felt neither joy nor sorrow at the little killing, but only acceptance—for he knew how many different deaths there were waiting for each young bird. They die of drought, and hailstones; they are abandoned by their parents when small boys reach in and touch; they fall prey to foxes, cats, stoats, weasels, rats, squirrels, magpies, crows, hawks and owls, at various stages of their growth . . . the old man knew that for every young blackbird that survives to take a mate, perhaps twenty more will die, one way or the other—so how could he feel bitterness, or even sorrow, at the death of one?

Towards the end of July there was a heat-wave. The temperature rose steadily until well into the eighties and then stayed there, day after day, while the land began to dry up. After a week there was a fine film of dust over everything—every leaf, every blade of grass, every wilting flower. Cracks appeared in the parched earth, like age wrinkles over a face. The water-table was way down and some of the smaller ponds were already dry.

Bird-song faltered, became desultory and finally almost ceased. Chaffinches still sang, but without joy. Sparrows made a subdued twittering that was as dry as the vegetation all around. Only one bird sang sweetly and defiantly from the parched hedgerows—it had been singing the same way since early spring, but its song had been swamped by the rest of the chorus; now it was alone. Sounding doubly sweet in the silence of the drought, the yellowhammers sang along the dusty lanes.

So, silence in the tree-tops; but just above ground-level a cheerful and industrious humming showed that the bees were carrying on as usual. The lean, ascetic hive-bees went everywhere in a short-tempered hurry, working as though time were running out before some imminent catastrophe. In direct contrast to their frenzy, the bumble-bees went booming calmly about their tasks, fat and amiable and fuzzy. The comparison between the frenetic city-dweller and his slow and rubicund country cousin is irresistible—yet bumble-bees are workers, nevertheless: they start work somewhere around 4 a.m. at this time of year, and on a clear moonlit night you can see them—or rather, hear them—still at work around midnight or even one o'clock in the morning.

Tag and Merlin took it easy, anyway. They became completely nocturnal, spending the days sleeping, somewhere in the woods; at night they prowled, played, and hunted, much as usual, except that it was dark. Foxhounds do not normally operate in the dark, but Merlin soon began to pick up the art of "seeing" with his nose and ears, and of remembering his surroundings in detail. He was becoming more of a fox every day.

Asher took to going out with hounds at 4 a.m. so as to get back before the heat really began. Even before dawn, men and animals were sweating heavily. The work of breaking up carcasses in the flesh-hovel became almost unbearable, but had to be done.

The harvest began before the weather broke, and Tag and Merlin had a day of unrelieved excitement when the combine harvesters moved into the field of barley near the kennels. They played havoc with the hordes of mice, voles and shrews that were disturbed by the great machines, and gorged until they could eat no more. For a while they went on, trying to bury their spoils, but at last they gave up, exhausted and content. That night the weather changed. The two animals were asleep in the wood when the temperature fell sharply and it started to rain. Merlin was woken by the dripping of large rain drops on to the briars in which they lay; after a period of anxiety, during which he became progressively wetter, he got up and set off for home and dry kennel. Tag opened one eye and watched him go; then, settling himself with his brush wrapped well over his nose for warmth, he went back to sleep, alone.

*   *   *

One day Merlin and Tag got into the huntsman's house. It was a Sunday and Asher had taken Cathie and Jenny to visit a relative. Jenny had run back to the house for her mother's handbag and left the back door open in her haste to get back to the waiting car. It was not long before Tag had discovered the inviting opening, but it was Merlin who plucked up the courage to lead the way in. After a brief period of nervous awe, the two animals began to relax and look around for possibilities. A game of hide-and-seek began which became more and more boisterous; soon it had degenerated into a free-for-all, which took them up the stairs and into Asher's bedroom; here a spirt of evil mischief seemed to invest them, for—as though intoxicated by the proximity of so much potential destruction— they started to take the place apart. Curtains went; sheets went and blankets, too; the stuffing was torn out of an old easy chair; everything went off Cathie's dressing table and one picture—a watercolor of Cleethorpes pier—was mysteriously dislodged from its place on the wall. When the possibilities seemed to be exhausted in the bedroom, they went back down the stairs—Merlin gaily carrying the remains of one of Asher's slippers in his mouth. The kitchen went next, and finally the living-room, approximately half the contents of each room ending up in the garden or somewhere around the kennels. They had to leave it there because the family came back.

While Cathie cried in her anger and frustration, Asher kept silent. He knew who had left the door open so that the culprits could get in and he would rather the two animals take the brunt of his wife's indignation than that Jenny should get it. He himself felt nothing more than a mild irritation at the extensive damage to their home: after all it was the nature of the animals and he knew it.

*   *   *

One night early in September, Tag and Merlin ran into a family group of four young foxes. It was a clear night, and a full moon lit everything with a cold brilliance. The wild cubs had been playing, romping exuberantly in the long grass beside a wood, but when they saw the two intruders they forgot their games. At first they all stood frozen, staring at each other, but after a while one of the wild foxes began to move forward, stiff-legged and on tip-toe, his hackles up. Three feet in front of Tag he stopped and they both began to growl, very quietly. After a minute or so of this they both lay down, still facing each other, their forelegs pushed out straight in front of them, their heads held high. All this time Merlin remained motionless, a few paces behind Tag. Suddenly the tension dissolved— for no evident reason. One of the other three, a female, walked over to Tag and sniffed at him, then performed a coquettish pirouette as an invitation to play. Cautiously at first the six animals played—not all together but in groups of two or three that shifted and changed as time passed. Gradually the play became more aggressive—the yaps and screams of the young foxes louder and angrier, and teeth began to hurt. It must have been on the point of degenerating into a full-scale battle when Mother arrived. With no warning a long shape hurtled out of the shadows and sent Merlin sprawling end over end with a yelp of dismay; Tag was already on his way at top speed and Merlin set off after him without waiting for further instructions. As they fled into the night they heard the vindictive *yap-yurr!* of the vixen behind them.

The following morning Asher saw Merlin licking his side fretfully. On closer inspection he saw that the young hound had a gash clean across his shoulder-blade. He took him into the kennels and treated the wound, then turned him loose again. Later that day Tag tried to lick the place and discovered that he didn't like the taste of antiseptic.

"How's that young hound making out?" Kendrick asked one evening.

"Merlin? Very nicely, as far as I can tell," Asher replied.

"How about that fox—are they still sticking together?"

Asher nodded.

"I'm afraid so. I don't know what to do about it, either."

"Don't let it bother you, Ash—it'll work itself out."

"I hope so!"

"Mind you, you'll have to lock the hound up whenever we're hunting anywhere in the district."

"Yes, of course; and Tag as well!" Kendrick shrugged.

"Well, that's not quite so important, but we can't have Merlin entering himself at the tender age of five months or so. It would hardly be good for discipline."

Asher wanted to smile at the thought, but he saw that Kendrick was being serious so he suppressed it. Later that evening, Jenny broached the same subject;

"Daddy, what's going to happen to Merlin and Tag when you're hunting?"

"Well . . . when we're over this side of the country I'll shut 'em up for the day."

"Tag, too?"

"Certainly—as long as I can get him in."

The answer seemed to satisfy her, but she had something else on her mind, for later she asked;

"How about next season?"

"How about it, then?"

"When Merlin's entered—what will you do with Tag then?"

"My dear girl, he'll be a wild fox by then and able to look after himself."

"But . . ." she was working up to the big question: "What'll happen if you find Tag one day and hunt him, and Merlin's in the pack—what will Merlin do? Will he hunt him, like all the others?"

Asher laughed.

"That's ridiculous," he said.

"But . . ."

"Get on with your homework, go on!"

But it wasn't ridiculous, and Asher knew it. That night, when he was making his final round of the kennels before going to bed, he saw Tag sniffing around the boiler-house and went over to him. The young fox greeted Asher perfunctorily and consented to being stroked for a moment or two, but he grew quickly bored of it and trotted off to continue his investigations.

Asher watched him go, frowning . . . we probably will hunt him, he thought—and what the hell *is* going to happen when we do?

In the autumn, Tag taught Merlin to enjoy apples and plums that lay rotting on the ground. By the time the last of the fruit had gone, winter had set in.

The two young animals had lost the last traces of babyhood; they were lean and hard and healthy. Merlin was sleek and well-muscled and Tag had grown a beautiful thick coat. The young fox was a fine specimen; his brush was full length now—long and bushy, with a white tip; his pointed face was framed in a silky ruff and his chest and underbelly were a rich cream. The streak above his eye where the hair grew white, as a result of his babyhood scar, was a certain identification mark and showed up clearly, even at a distance—a point noticed by Tod, who continued to observe them, regardless of the weather.

The nights began to turn cold. Apart from the odd day when Merlin was locked up in the kennels, because they were hunting nearby, the hound and the fox were inseparable companions. One thing was very noticeable, however; they hardly ever played. During the summer, anything between five and ten hours had been spent in play of one kind or another, but now they seemed to have grown up, all of a sudden.

Although Asher still put down food for them without fail, they did not rely on it. They were hunting more assiduously and farther afield every day now. Even their hunting, during the mild summer evenings, had involved a strong element of fun, but now it was deadly serious and very much a team operation.

The Foxhound/Houndfox syndrome appeared to be almost complete, and both animals would switch from one role to the other as quickly and as easily as blinking. Walking quietly through the woods one day, Merlin put up a pheasant. As the big bird rocketed almost vertically upwards, the hound leaped to intercept it, twisted with the agility of a fox and caught it by one wing. When he and Tag had eaten it, they both turned and left their scent on the pile of feathers, which was all that remained of the bird. This was normal fox procedure: a method of stating ownership, or a territorial claim. But what was significant about it was that Merlin performed the same ritual—yet it is not a foxhound habit. When Tod came across the double-autographed pile of feathers, some hours later, he stood there for a long time, staring in silent wonder.

And the other way round, too: when Tag found the fresh line of a rabbit, he surged forward, breathing in deeply until he was sure of it, then gave a sharp yelp to call Merlin, who came running. Together they hunted the line, with mounting excitement as it grew stronger and fresher in their nostrils—and when, in his enthusiasm, Merlin drove on over the line as it turned sharply, it was Tag whose head swung to the left—Tag who went back to check—and Tag who proclaimed the correct line with a derisive yap as Merlin hesitated and feathered... The old man did not witness this incident, but it would only have confirmed what he knew already in his heart: that he was seeing something extraordinary, if not unique, in this relationship between two creatures—two animals who were born to be enemies, yet had grown so close they were in the process of merging, one into the other.

As he watched them living and hunting together through the long winter, Tod came to believe that he was witnessing some kind of miracle.

Chapter Eight

ASHER DELAYED IT as long as he dared, but at last he could postpone it no longer: on the first of April he called Merlin into the kennels and put him in with the young hounds, back from walk.

For almost a week the nights were hideous with Merlin's howling and Tag's eerie screaming and yapping. In the end Asher had to go out and chase the fox away—much against his will—because Cathie could not sleep.

After that the noise abated, but for weeks Tag was a forlorn figure, haunting the kennels like a russet ghost. Every morning Asher saw the damp footprints of the fox where he had walked up and down, up and down, like a sentry outside the yard in which Merlin was imprisoned—for Asher did not dare take him out, knowing that he would lose him.

So, while Merlin's contemporaries began their training, walking out every day with Asher and Stephen, the young hound stayed in the kennels, locked in. After a while he started to lose flesh; his coat had a lifeless look about it and his eyes were sunken and brooding. Asher felt miserable every time he saw him, but he knew that he had to see it through. It was too late to turn back.

At last the turning point came—for the first time in more than six weeks, there were no footprints outside Merlin's prison. A few days later Asher was certain; Tag had finally given up and drifted away.

That afternoon Merlin went out on exercise for the first time. He was coupled to a steady old hound as a precaution, but it was not really necessary; he simply jogged along listlessly and hardly even bothered to look around. After that he began the slow climb back to health.

By the time mounted hound exercise started, at the end of June, Merlin looked to be more or less back to normal; he went out with the pack as a matter of course, but Asher felt a pang of misery—and perhaps of guilt—every time he looked at him, for he went like an old hound; head and hindquarters low, feet dragging. It was even worse when Asher spoke to him in kennel: Merlin would respond to his name and came forward when called, but when Asher looked into his eyes he saw only a smoldering opaqueness which denied him entry. Of all the hounds that Asher had known and loved he grew to love Merlin more than any other, partly because of this. He imagined the misery, the ache of separation in the dim animal brain, and as he watched the young hound climb back on to the bench and lie down apathetically, facing the wall, he experienced a feeling of desolation.

"Perhaps it'll be all right when he starts hunting," he told Cathie that night, in a rare moment of confidence.

"It's upsetting you properly, isn't it?" she said.

"I can't help it—I feel responsible."

"But it's not your fault, love."

"It's not a question of fault, it's a question of responsibility, and that's mine."

"He'll be all right, Asher, I'm sure he will."

"Perhaps he'll be all right when he starts hunting," he murmured, unaware that he was repeating himself.

"Yes, I expect he will," Cathie said.

*　　*　　*

Merlin was showing just enough slow improvement to keep Asher hopeful for the future. Although the look in his eyes never changed the young hound was beginning to show a little more interest when out with the pack.

Training was proceeding normally—the young hounds had to learn the elementary disciplines of life in a pack of fox-hounds: like going to the huntsman when he calls them; like leaving "riot" alone—that is, rabbit, hare, deer, etc.; like simple good manners towards people and dogs; road-discipline, and so on. The young entry also had to learn how to contain their exuberance and defer to the older and more experienced hounds.

All of this Merlin took in his stride; in fact, he assimilated it too easily for Asher's liking. He found himself wishing that the young hound would show just one spark of disobedience or initiative—anything, so long as it broke the continuing apathy in which he lived, and whose shell Asher could not even crack.

August saw them riding out for up to three or four hours every morning, then walking out for another hour and a half in the evenings. Their muscles were hard and so were their pads, after twenty-odd miles a day on the tarmac. The hunters were up by this time as well, and getting almost as much exercise as the hounds. The horses used by Asher and Stephen for hound-exercise were retired hunters and were kept for this purpose; they also did the early cub-hunting days, and then went out to grass again when the hunt-horses took over, early in October.

Kendrick often joined Asher when he walked hounds out in the evening, and his heart always stirred with pleasure at the sight of the close-knit pack clustering around the slight figure of the huntsman in his dazzling white kennel-coat. Part of the old park had been left unploughed and when the evenings were sunny and warm they would walk out across the ancient turf and stand under one of the giant oak trees. At such a time Asher would allow pack-discipline to relax for a while so that the hounds could rest or go foraging, just as they pleased. From time to time he would call them, and they would fly to him from all directions and cluster round him as he spoke to them by name and threw pieces of biscuit. Kendrick would watch them— their coats gleaming in the sun-dappled shade, healthy, obedient and beautiful—and think himself lucky to be out with them on a summer evening. His wife had loved the hounds, too, and would often walk out with them; the hounds had adored her, for she had a wonderful quiet way and was not sloppy with them. He remembered the way she would always make a point of befriending the nervous hounds, not making a direct approach, but gradually drifting closer until she was able to use her voice—not looking at the hound, but into the distance, while she spoke to it, gently—and in the end she always won. He remembered Streamlet, who only ever went to two people in her life, as far as he knew; his wife and Asher. He remembered the hours she had spent in a grass yard with the frightened female reading a book and talking from time to time in a quiet voice, still without looking at her. He remembered her imperious gesture to him to keep away when he had approached, and the two little lines between her eyebrows as she asked for his indulgence with her eyes... Asher stole a glance at him and looked away again hurriedly, feeling as though he had committed an intrusion. When Kendrick had not moved, five minutes later, Asher called the hounds and the sudden movement brought him back to the present.

Waling back towards the kennels one evening, Kendrick asked:

"Seen anything of your fox lately Ash?"

"No, sir, not for a long time now."

"Well, that seems to have solved itself then."

"I hope so."

"And how about Merlin?"

Asher pulled his bowler back and rubbed his forehead with one hand—a gesture he often used when puzzled or worried.

"I don't know. I really don't know. He seems to miss his pal, even now, but I think he'll be all right when we start hunting."

"Think he'll enter all right?"

"I can't say. You can never tell, you know—the puppy you expect most of won't stoop to fox and the one you'd thought of leaving at home enters like an old hand. You just can't tell—at least, I never can."

"If you can't Ash, then I don't know anyone who could."

"I wouldn't say that, sir."

"I know you wouldn't."

During the first week in September Asher decided to teach the young hounds to keep away from sheep—a vital discipline, for every hunt depends on the goodwill of its farmers. Having laid it on with one of the tenants, he took the hounds to his farm, the next day. As they walked through the gate into the grass field, the sheep bunched up and stood staring at them suspiciously, in the far corner.

"Watch out now," Asher said quietly to Stephen.

"Right, sir."

The young whipper-in took up station on the flank, between the hounds and the sheep. As Asher walked slowly forward they both watched the young hounds carefully. The hounds sensed the tension and packed a little closer together. The experienced ones took one look at the sheep and knew what it was all about: they walked quietly forward with their heads turned a little away from the sheep, looking studiously anywhere but in their direction. The young hounds, on the other hand, had never seen sheep before, and were naturally curious. Most of them looked in their direction, and one or two of them started edging across towards them. Suddenly a young hound called Tester broke away from the body of the pack to go and investigate—he had taken no more than three steps when the thong of Stephen's whip cracked across his ribs and the young man's voice lashed him;

"'Ware sheep, Tester! 'Ware sheep, sir!"

The chastened hound leaped back into the middle of the throng, his tail between his legs. The whip cracked again:

"Ravish! 'Ware sheep!"

And again:

"Wilful! Have a care!"

And Asher walked slowly forward, chirruping quietly and reassuringly as the whipper-in punished where necessary and warned where necessary. At first the young hounds who had received a crack of the whip were upset and puzzled, but after a while they began to understand what was required of them, led on by the example of the old hounds, who walked stolidly forward, looking away from the sheep; soon, reassured by Asher's quiet voice, they began to learn.

After walking them up and down past the flock, a little nearer each time, Asher said, "That'll do for today," and took them home.

Every day for a while they went through the same performance until, in the end, Asher could hold them within a few yards of the sheep and see them all—every one of them—turn their backs on them as though there were no such thing.

"I think that'll do them," Asher said at last.

"It ought to," Stephen replied.

As they walked home, Asher realized that not once during the whole week had Merlin shown a single sign of disobedience—or, indeed, of anything else. He felt a depression settling over him—he knew it to be out of all proportion to get so involved with one hound out of eighty or so, but it was beyond his control. He so wanted Merlin to do well and dreaded the thought of what he must do should the young hound fail to come around.

The first day's cub-hunting was set for the second Tuesday in September. On the Monday afternoon, Asher drew his pack for the following day.

This was always one of the most difficult jobs of the year. He had to take as many young hounds as he could, for one of the purposes of cubbing was to teach young hounds how to hunt the fox—but if he took too many, control might be difficult. Then he had to take along as many good, steady hounds as he could—for by their example they would help the youngsters. These thoughts were at the back of his mind as he walked the hounds that evening, reviewing the merits of each one in turn. By the time they were back at the kennels he knew which hounds he wanted. With the whole pack massed in the Draw-yard, he went to the door that led into the court reserved for the pack that was to hunt the next day. He part-opened the door and stood in the opening, holding it with his left hand. Every hound was watching him expectantly as he stood surveying them, reviewing them, reviewing his decision one last time—then he was ready.

"Actor," he said, quietly.

An old dog-hound, grizzled and scarred from five seasons' hunting, moved forward towards

Asher, pushing his way carefully through the packed bodies.

"Cruiser."

As Actor reached him, Asher opened the door just enough to let him through; as the old hound brushed past his legs Asher touched him on the back with his whip—for no reason, other than that he had done it this way for over twenty years, and the hounds expected it. Meanwhile Cruiser was pushing his way through, towards him.

"Warrior."

And so on; each hound moving forward immediately its name was spoken, while the rest awaited their turn, unquestioningly; each hound touched on the back by Asher's whip as it passed through; until at last there were thirty-seven hounds inside the court.

Asher closed the door.

"Eighteen and a half couple," he said to Stephen.

"Yes, sir."

"Right. Let's get these put away then."

Later that evening Tod called in for his instructions.

An earth-stopper's job is to stop earths. He goes, silently, to the covers or thickets to be drawn the following day. He goes after sunset, when foxes are out and about at their various pursuits. He then blocks the entrance to any earth in that particular wood, or spinney, or gorse, and leaves as quietly as he came. When the fox returns, towards dawn, it finds its earth blocked. Not too disturbed, it finds a dry place nearby and settles down to sleep. When hounds arrive the fox can be hunted, for it is unable to take refuge in its earth. Later on in the season, the earth-stopper's task is more arduous, for he has to try to stop every earth over a large tract of country—and all between darkness and dawn, or he will stop the foxes inside their earths. The night after hunting he must unblock them again, so that the foxes can continue to use them. No wonder Tod was used to being out at night—he had adapted so completely to a nocturnal life that he could not have slept before dawn if he had tried. He always went to bed soon after daylight and slept for four hours exactly. He would then get up and cook himself a meal. After this he would doze in an armchair for perhaps an hour or two, and would then wake up properly and start on his chores. Whether he was actually stopping earths or not he was always out in the country at night, and it was because of this that he knew the whereabouts and movements of almost every fox in the district.

That evening he was dressed, as always, in his long overcoat, with a scarf round his throat and woollen mittens which left his calloused fingers free. Traditionally, earth-stoppers carried lanterns, and many modern ones take a powerful torch, but not Tod. By day his eyesight was not particularly good, but by night all his senses combined to such a focus of concentration that he could find his way, even on the darkest night, across the wildest parts of the country.

Asher sat him down in his usual chair and poured him a cup of tea. Tod took a sip and nodded appreciatively as Asher sat down on the other side of the fire.

"Burnetts tomorrow, then?" Tod asked.

"Aye, and perhaps Hartwell Gorse."

"Ye'll not get there, will yer?"

Asher shrugged.

"I might. It's pretty thick in Burnetts, is it?"

"Thicker'n I've ever seen it."

"Then we might have to stop there. How many in there?"

"Two litters; three brace and two and a half brace."

Asher nodded.

"Should be all right. A lot of brambles?"

"Aye, a fair bit."

The huntsman frowned.

"That's a pity," he muttered. "I don't like 'em getting too torn about the first day."

They were silent for a while, each occupied with his own thoughts. Then Tod spoke again:

"Are yer taking Merlin?"

"Aye."

"Is he all right now?"

"I'll tell you tomorrow night."

The old man nodded, understanding immediately that Asher didn't want to talk about it.

"Is that fox around?" Asher asked, after a silence.

"Not where you're goin' tomorrow."

"But he is around somewhere?"

The old man nodded and put his empty glass in the hearth.

"Tod..." Asher began, then hesitated. The old man cocked a bushy eyebrow at him, waiting. Asher went on: "Is he all right? I mean, is he looking after himself all right?"

Tod exploded with a snort of derisive laughter.

"All right?" he almost shouted. "'Course he's all right! He's a fox, ain't he?"

Asher looked relieved.

"It was a stupid question," he said, with a wry grin. The old man stood up with a grunt.

"I'll be on me way," he said.

Asher went to the door with him and stepped outside to look at the weather. The sky was overcast and there was a cool north-westerly breeze. Tod sniffed at the moving air, raising his shaggy head and turning it a little from side to side, like an old boar badger.

"I'll keep dry tonight," he said, "and so will you tomorrow."

He moved off down the path. Asher, watching

the bear-like figure shambling away into the night, saw him stop and turn.

"Good luck for tomorrow," the old man said, out of the darkness.

Chapter Nine

WHEN HE HAD finally got over his separation from Merlin, Tag moved on. Something made him travel on without stopping until he found himself in country that was strange to him—country that he had never visited with Merlin. It would be hard to say why he did this. An animal would not consciously leave a district in order to avoid memories which might be painful—that is a human reaction; animals don't work that way. Whatever the reason, he made straight for fresh country and finally adopted Hungarton Wood as his home base.

Young foxes normally live above ground, and Tag was no exception; he had four or five different "couches" where he could sleep dry with a clear area around him in case danger threatened. His life with Merlin had been virtually that of a wild fox, and in April there is plenty of food to be had for the picking. There were other foxes in Hungarton Wood, but it was a big covert and they left him alone. Only once was he attacked, and that was when he went too close to an occupied earth; the vixen found him sniffing at it, scenting the cubs inside, and flew at him. He escaped with nothing more than a few scratches and his wounded pride, and after that he left other foxes' earths alone.

As the summer went by, memories of life at the kennels slipped further and further into the background—yet one link with the past remained, for someone had followed Tag to his new home.

Tod had always been interested in foxes, as a matter of course; but with the advent of Tag he stopped watching foxes and started watching just one. At first, after Merlin's return the kennels and the consequent splitting-up of the partnership, the old man had felt lost. Following and watching the two young animals had given him a feeling of purpose, and more than that—for they had become, in a sense, the children he had never had. During the weeks when Tag padded and howled around the kennels, Tod grieved with him; and when Tag moved on, the old man was never far behind.

That summer, Tod's attitude towards the young fox underwent a subtle change and began to develop in a new direction. Watching Tag and Merlin together in Kennel Wood, he had been observing and learning, more than anything else; but now that Tag was on his own, some sympathetic chord was struck with the old man's lifelong feeling of solitude, and he began to experience something approaching love for the young fox. Throughout the summer he spent most of his time in and around Hungarton Wood. Imperceptibly, the invisible thread that stretched between them grew shorter, and Tag began to play an increasingly important role in the old man's life, for by now he was living *through* the wild animal; sharing in his failures and triumphs; feeling hunger and thirst and fatigue and even pain through the animal's senses rather than his own.

Some of Tod's happiest experiences that summer were the times he watched Tag hunting for mice—usually around dusk.

To see a fox mouse-hunting is to see one of the most appealing sights possible—they are such graceful animals. Tag would creep quietly across the meadow until he came to a likely spot, then stand absolutely still, his ears pricked forward, listening intently. The small rodents that live in meadows move along runs—little tunnels in the grass—so that they cannot be seen. But they can be heard; the traffic along these tunnels is pretty heavy, especially around this time of year, and shrews being what they are—which is highly emotional—fights break out all over the place. These fights are accompanied by frenzied squeaking, and it was this commotion that Tag would listen for. When he heard the high furious shouts of a couple of battling shrews he would take a fix on the spot with his sensitive ears, creep forward, then rear up on his hind-legs and come down stiff-legged, with both front paws together, right on top of the shrews. Apart from filling his stomach, it was highly entertaining sport, and this is always an important factor for a well-fed fox.

Autumn came with its crop of berries and rotting fruit beneath the trees in the orchards. Tag continued to live well and easily, yet Tod noticed something about him . . . hard to define, yet definitely there. He wore a "lost" look much of the time, when he would wander aimlessly round the country, searching for he knew not what. Although he had adapted far more readily to wild life than had Merlin to life in the kennels, he had not forgotten the young hound. It was as though they had become Siamese twins during the days when they had fought together, back-to-back, against overwhelming odds—and now separated by force, neither was quite complete—each was fated to live as best he could while searching, always searching, for the missing piece.

Chapter Ten

ASHER CHECKED HIS girth and settled his stirrup leathers, then patted the old horse on the neck.

"All right, Frank," he called. He heard the clang as the kennelman drew the bolt and the next moment the door opened and the hounds flooded out. In the early morning darkness, he could see only the white markings on the hounds—their muzzles and legs and hindquarters, and those few with odd white markings on their bodies. His horse tensed suddenly and sidled as the hounds pressed round its legs, but it did not kick—a huntsman's horse must never kick, and Heather had been a huntsman's horse for fourteen years. Asher squeezed her with his legs and she walked forward obediently, trembling with suppressed excitement.

"Co-ope!" he called to his hounds. "Cope then!"

They surged forward around his horse, panting with eagerness. One or two of them gave muffled *woofs*, but guiltily, fully aware that it was frowned upon. As they walked round the front of the kennels, Asher saw a dim shape moving out to one side, across the grass. Even as he turned to warn Stephen he saw a larger shape move up behind the first one. There was a muffled crack and a yelp, and he heard a voice:

"Traitor! Get on back to 'em."

Asher smiled in the darkness: after two seasons, the young man was beginning to do his job without being told.

They moved out on to the road and Asher urged the mare forward into a steady trot. He could hear the pattering of the hound's feet on the wet road between the horses' ringing hoofbeats, and the whisper of their breathing. He looked ahead and saw the road shining like a ribbon of silver where it reflected the growing radiance in the dawn sky. The air was damp and cool against his cheek and rich with the smells of the autumn countryside. He felt the great lift and soaring of his heart that always accompanied this moment of the day—when all the things he loved most deeply came suddenly into conjunction.

Asher heard a faint yelp and turned to see a tail-ender galloping hastily forward from Stephen's whip. Without slowing down he called out:

"Give them more law, Stephen—they've got to have chance to empty themselves."

"Sorry, sir," Stephen called and dropped farther back.

In spite of his apparently cheerful compliance with the huntsman's order, Stephen had to fight a new desire to answer back. Although he accepted the rigorous discipline that went with his chosen profession, it was not without a struggle—and a continuing one, at that—for as well as being young and intelligent, Stephen Durno was also ambitious. It was not altogether his fault, for he came from a famous hunting family, and several of his ancestors had been renowned huntsmen. Stephen was determined to create his own niche in the halls of fame, and was going at it with all the fire and impatience of youth. But in the long apprenticeship that was necessary to learn the job, impatience was an uncomfortable attribute, and after only two years, Stephen was beginning to fret and champ at the bit. Asher was aware of all this, but said nothing. As far as he was concerned, it was Stephen's problem, not his—and that is not to say that he was unsympathetic, for he remembered his own long apprenticeship as whipper-in to his father. But *he* had been left to sort it out for himself, and now he was going to leave it to Stephen. The young man would either come through it with his character tempered by the fire, or he would fall by the wayside... and in their profession, it was stamina that told, in the end.

Forty minutes after leaving the kennels, they turned off the road and up a track towards the low-lying mass of Burnetts Wood, showing purple across the fields. Kendrick was already there, mounted on his aging gray—they had traveled by Land-Rover and trailer, to save the horse's legs and the Master's seat-bones. Asher went straight to him and saluted him, then took the hounds over to the hedge and took up his position there, with Stephen to one side, watching them carefully. Two other people were already there, and another twenty-five or thirty arrived during the next ten minutes—only four of them mounted, the rest on foot. As they turned up, they greeted the Master first and then the Hunt servants, after which they stood and talked in groups. It was fully light by now, and the air was warming up. Asher hoped that it would not get too hot, for everybody's sake.

At five-forty-five exactly, Kendrick looked at his watch.

"Very well, Asher," he said.

Asher nodded and moved forward towards one end of the wood—the end that was downwind; at the same time, Kendrick took the "field" and began to station them at intervals round the edge of the wood. Asher waited while the covert was being surrounded, holding his hounds about thirty yards from its edge. As soon as the process was complete he waved his arm towards the wood:

"Leu in, my beauties! Leu in, then," he called.

The hounds who had hunted before surged forward in a body and flung themselves into the wood, leaving the young hounds standing, staring in amazement and looking up at Asher for help. He walked forward, smiling.

"Leu in, then! Leu in, babies," he crooned, urging them forward. One or two of them caught on and dashed forward after the old hounds, but the remainder stayed at his side, their expressions a picture of consternation.

He entered the wood and walked on along a ride with most of the young hounds still clustered round him. He turned to Stephen.

"Go ahead and put yourself where the rides cross," he said. "Make as little noise as you can—If I'm nearby when he crosses, then tell me. If I'm not then keep it to yourself. Off you go."

The whipper-in trotted past eagerly. Young Truman followed him for a little way, then stopped and looked back guiltily, as though expecting to be punished for leaving Asher's side. The huntsman smiled again.

"You'll learn," he said.

There is always this problem for young hounds when first they go hunting ever since returning from walk, they have learned to stick close to the huntsman—now suddenly they are being encouraged to leave his side and dash off into the woods where the older hounds are already having a lot of fun, by the sound of it. The naughty ones, the wilful and mischievous ones always go first, for it is in their nature—but the obedient ones, the solid and reliable ones are thunderstruck at this *lèse-majesté*; they stay by the huntsman's side and stare at him with horrified expressions. Asher never could keep a straight face when they looked up at him like that, but he did not laugh at them.

"Never mind, my babies, it'll come," he told them.

From somewhere in the depths of the wood came a whimper. Asher froze, straining his ears. Then another and then a deeper note. *Ardent*, he thought. *Good old dog.* The next moment there was a crash of hound-music which rang from end to end of the covert, and swelled as more and more hounds owned the line and joined in. He looked down and saw the young hounds staring towards the sound, ears pricked and heads on one side. As he watched, another three hounds dashed forward and plunged into the undergrowth, leaving him with four and a half couple. No, he thought, as he turned to look behind: five couple—for Merlin was standing behind him, not even looking towards the thrilling sound at the heart of the wood. He fought down a feeling of disappointment, then turned back as the music faltered and died away. He walked forward and started to cheer his hounds in a clear, high-pitched voice:

"Yoi try! Yoi try-hy! Yoi rouse 'em there!"

He blew a couple of short notes on his horn, then a couple more as the cry faltered and ceased.

"Yoi try-hy!"

He heard a whimper, then the querulous half-bark, half-howl which is the foxhound's voice when it owns a fox's line. He recognized it instantly.

"Yoi at 'im, Ruin!" he cheered. "Hark to Ruin! Hark 'ark 'ark to Ruin!"

More voices were thrown in, and still more, until once again the woods were echoing and re-echoing the sound. The fox was running round the perimeter of the wood, with the body of the pack about fifty yards behind it. Asher caught a movement from the corner of his eye and turned like lightning, just in time to see a well-grown fox-cub cross the ride in front of him, and not twenty yards away. Not one of the young hounds had seen it, he noticed—they were all straining towards the sound of the hunt. As he watched, another young hound suddenly broke away from him and galloped away down the ride towards its companions. His heart leaped for a moment, but it was not Merlin.

For over an hour the hunt went on, round and round the big wood. Asher estimated that there were two or two and a half brace of cubs in there. An old fox had been seen slipping away down a hedgerow as hounds were being put in and Asher had not seen another, so he guessed the remainder to be all cubs.

Although still known as "cubs," young foxes are, by this time, well-grown. Apart from its function of "entering" young hounds, cub-hunting has two more important aims. The first is to teach young foxes to "run." They are hunted round and round the covert until at last they leave it and make a dash for it across open country—at this stage of the season, they are allowed to escape, and this success teaches them an important lesson: when hounds are put in, get out and go! The second aim is to kill some foxes. When the only foxes left in covert are those who are unwilling to risk it in the open, the huntsman will hope to kill them—for this, after all, is what the whole thing is about. Hunting is a method of control; indeed, as far as the naturalist is concerned, it is the best method, for it keeps foxes down to a sensible level without threatening to wipe out the whole population. During cubbing the bold, strong young foxes get away, while the weaker foxes are killed—and in this sense it is also a form of natural selection, ensuring that most of the best specimens survive and go on to breed.

Asher heard a new note of excitement under the cry of the hounds, and then a sudden silence that left the woods echoing.

"They've killed him," he said to no one, and

urged the mare forward into a canter. He shouted to Stephen to follow him and plunged into the dense undergrowth. Thirty seconds later he found them: two of the young hounds were still pulling at the very dead corpse, but the rest were standing around panting, or even lying down—for it was getting hot in the wood. Asher dismounted—swinging his leg forward over the pommel as he always did—and walked over to take the corpse from the two youngsters.

"Who-hoop!" he yelled, and again, "who-hoop!" He took the horn from its place between the first and second buttons of his hunting-coat and blew the long, tremulous note of the "kill." Then he encouraged the hounds, praising them in a cheerful voice, until Stephen rode up. The whipper-in took the corpse from him and started to break it up, and Asher walked back to his mount, who was standing exactly where he had left her. He mounted, blew a brief note on the horn to call hounds to him, and set off towards the ride. As soon as most of them were with him he waved them in to draw again.

"Leu in! Leu in, then!"

This time, he noticed with satisfaction, only three hounds stayed with him. He glanced at them and his heart leaped as he saw that Merlin was not among them. "Haw!" he exclaimed.

By this time they had been round the covert so many times that it was badly foiled; it was getting hot, too, and there was little scent, so Asher decided to give up. The hounds were pretty tired by now, and most of them were badly torn about the face and ears by brambles. When they had broken up the second cub Asher started to blow his horn to call the stragglers in, and set off along the ride. By the time he had left the wood, most of the hounds were with him. He turned and started to make* them, but

* Count.

Stephen called out, "Sixteen couple, sir."

Asher nodded. He halted and went on blowing the long call-notes on the horn, while Stephen went back into the covert, calling the stragglers. One by one the remaining hounds emerged from the edge of the wood and came trotting or cantering up. Asher looked inquiringly at Stephen.

"Eighteen couple, sir."

"Who's missing?"

"Merlin, I think."

Asher's heart sank—he knew immediately what had happened, but he blew his horn and called for another five minutes, just in case he were wrong.

Kendrick rode up; everyone else had gone home.

"Missing one?" he asked.

"Yes, sir."

"Which one?"

"Merlin."

"Oh . . ." Kendrick was saddened; he had an idea of Asher's involvement with the young hound and could guess at the huntsman's feelings at that moment.

"Well," he said, trying to sound cheerful. "He'll probably be waiting for you when you get back."

"Yes, sir," Asher said dutifully, but neither of them believed it.

When they got back to the kennels Merlin wasn't there, nor did he arrive during the long afternoon. As he stood looking down at the feeding hounds, Asher knew that he should be feeling content with the morning's business, but his heart was heavy and the joy had gone out of it all. Frank Sammells and Stephen saw him brooding and left him alone, knowing that they could do nothing to help.

As soon as he had exercised and put away the hounds who hadn't been hunting that day, Asher changed his clothes and went off in the car to look for Merlin. He took Jenny with him and was glad of her company because her unvarying optimism buoyed him up as their search continued unsuccessful. He drove for miles in the general area of Burnetts, asking everyone they met, but no one had seen the solitary hound. At last it began to get dark and he turned for home.

"He'll be all right, Daddy," Jenny said, "I know he will."

"Yes, my love."

"No," she insisted, almost angrily, "I really mean it!"

He was affected by the passion in her voice—he put his hand on her knee and squeezed:

"You're a good kid," he said.

That evening he made an effort to rise above his depression. For a while he made himself talk to Cathie—about Kendrick, about Jenny's schooling, about redecorating the house... about anything except what was troubling him. Cathie knew that something was wrong and her heart warmed towards him, knowing that he was trying for her sake, more than his own. She sat in the chair opposite him, knitting a pullover for Jenny, and as he talked she tried, too—tried to be warm and sympathetic to maintain the balm of idle chat. At last he fell silent and sat gazing into the fire, absolutely still. She looked at his profile and saw the lines etched deep from his nostrils to the corners of his mouth, giving his expression a touch of bitterness. It was only at moments like this, when Asher withdrew completely into his inner world, that his wife could really look at him. Without her knowledge her hands slowed down and finally stopped half-way through a stitch as she looked at him, drinking in every feature, every line of his face in one unremitting draught—he turned suddenly and looked at her, and she was aware all at once of the picture she must present; leaning forward, wide-eyed, her knitting arrested in her hands. His deep-set grey eyes seemed to burn through her—she looked down hurriedly at her hands and started to knit again, feeling the hot flush spread over her face and down her neck. She knitted furiously for what must have been minutes on end before risking a quick glance: he was looking into the fire again, as though he had never moved. She waited until her composure had returned, then put her knitting down, got up and went over to him. She touched his shoulder gently and said, "I'll do your chocolate, Asher." Without looking up he raised his hand and pressed her fingers down on to his shoulder.

"And you're a good kid, too," he said. She didn't understand the phrasing, but when she went out to put the milk on there was a ball of happiness in her throat that made her quite breathless for a minute or two.

Before going up to bed, Asher went out into the silent night. He stood out on the grass in front of the kennels and listened to the night-sounds; the distant quavering hoot of a tawny owl, the squeak and rustle of bats, a hound dreaming on its bed of straw. He put his hands into the pockets of his dressing-gown and walked round the side and into the kennels themselves. His slippered feet made no sound, yet still they heard him—he sensed the sudden lifting of heads and cocking of ears—would have worried if he hadn't, in fact, for it meant that everything was normal ... apart from the one thing that wasn't. It was not until he felt the wave of disappointment break over him that he realized that he had expected Merlin to be there.

He went to bed, fell into a deep sleep somewhere around two o'clock and woke with a start just before five. Feeling confused and—for some reason—angry, he got out of bed and pulled some clothes on. He was calmer by the time he walked out of the back door into the kennels, but he still didn't know what had woken him. When he saw the dark shape by the wall in the Draw-yard, he felt no surprise.

He walked slowly over to where Merlin was sitting on his haunches and stopped in front of him.

"Merlin," he said quietly.

The young hound's rear moved a couple of times, just an inch or two each way, and was still again. Asher sat down in front of him, his back resting against the brick wall. He reached out and fondled him around his ears and throat.

"Merlin," he said again.

The hound looked at him for a moment, and then looked away again. Asher didn't need daylight to know the expression in the amber eyes—he knew it already. He felt despair wash over him, so soon after the relief of seeing the hound back again. He took Merlin's head in both his hands and turned it towards him so that the young hound's eyes could no longer avoid his.

"Merlin," he whispered, "what's the matter? Where are you? I can't get to you, I can't find you. What can I do? you can't go on mourning for ever, for God's sake..."

The shadowed eyes seemed to be looking steadily into his, but he could not tell whether or not the young hound was seeing him.

"If only there were something I could do..." he whispered, then let his hands fall away. As soon as he felt himself free again, Merlin turned away and sat in the same position as before—head hanging, looking down at the floor. Feeling heavy with failure, Asher got up stiffly.

"Come on, then." he said wearily and turned towards the door. Merlin walked into the yard and stood patiently while Asher opened the door into the lodging-room, then walked into that without a murmur. Asher heard the quick rustle as hounds moved to identify the late-comer, then silence again.

The leaves withered and began to fall, blown away by the cold easterly winds. Cubbing continued normally with only one fault to mar the general picture: Merlin's continued refusal to "enter." In the end Asher managed to get the young hound to leave his side and go into covert, but he would not draw— he mostly wandered around until it was time to go, then joined on again. He took absolutely no interest in what was going on all round him, and once Asher found him lying down, resting. By the time they had started to let hounds run, early in October, Kendrick was showing signs of restlessness.

"Still persevering with that hound?" he asked, one evening.

"Yes, sir."

"You still think he'll enter?"

"I'm not sure."

"Well then..." Kendrick felt embarrassed. "Don't you think it's time you gave up then? Can't have him holding the others back."

"He won't do that, sir."

"All right, if you say so."

"Thank you, sir."

Asher was always so infuriatingly polite when he was sticking his heels in, Kendrick thought angrily.

Other people noticed, too. In fact it was hard to avoid noticing. One night Frank Sammells and Stephen Durno were having a drink at the local when Tod walked in and sat down beside them. After a little desultory conversation there was a silence, then Stephen came out with it:

"How about our huntsman then?" he said.

"What d'yer mean?" Tod asked. Frank shot

Stephen a warning look but the lad missed it—he was very slightly tight, which was unusual.

"Mooning about the place over his favorite," Stephen went on, "waiting for the miracle to happen."

Tod's voice was dangerously friendly.

"What miracle?" he asked softly.

"You know perfectly well what I mean."

"Now then, Steve," Frank said, warningly, but the young man had the bit between his teeth and was talking animatedly, his face flushed and his eyes shining:

"That hound, Tod, you know the one I mean— that Merlin. Honestly, what's he doing taking it day after day? That hound isn't going to enter—not in a month of Sundays!"

"And what would you do?" Tod asked, in the same soft voice.

"Draft him. Knock him on the head. Anything except go on taking him out where he can have a bad effect on the rest of the hounds! You know why Asher won't give up? Because he let Merlin chum up with that fox, that's why, and now he doesn't want to admit that it was a mistake! That hound's never been any good since Tag went, and what's more, he—"

"Stephen—" Frank warned, but it was too late. Both men jumped as Tod's huge mittened fist crashed down on the tabletop, making the beer-mugs rock. The old man thrust his head forward, his old reptilian eyes glittering with anger.

"Listen, you blown-up young toad," he hissed, impaling the startled young man on a finger like a small log, "you're working under a man who's forgotten more about hounds than you'll ever know. What's more, he's straight—straight as a die—and one thing you won't find him doing is talking about you behind your back!"

Stephen's pleasant young face flushed a deeper shade—he tried to hold the old man's look, but failed.

"I don't think you—" he started, then broke off. Moments later he stood up, pushing his chair back violently, turned and walked quickly out of the bar with Tod glaring at his back all the way. The moment the door had closed behind him the old man relaxed and reached for his mug.

"That wasn't very kind," Frank said, sharply for him. Tod stopped and stared at the kennelman in amazement.

"Not very kind?"

"He's a good lad, Tod—he's just had a pint too many—it was the beer talking, you know that."

"I don't care what it was talking, I'll listen to no one being clever about Asher Smith," Tod growled.

"But he worships Asher."

"Then he's a funny manner o' showing it," Tod flared.

Frank shook his head sadly and said nothing. After a minute or two, Tod drained his mug, stood up and walked out without another word.

The funny thing is that Stephen was not far from the truth, for Asher was in the depths of despair about Merlin's continued refusal to enter—in fact, he was on the verge of giving up.

There were three more cubbing Meets to go before the Opening Meet. Without making any conscious decision, Asher left Merlin at home for the first two of them. What made him decide to give the young hound a last chance, he could not afterwards recall. All he knew was that when he had chosen his pack from the Draw-yard, the evening before the last of the three Meets, he looked into the court and saw that Merlin was in there with them. He was astonished, because he couldn't remember calling him, but he was too superstitious to pull him out again, so there he stayed. The following morning dawned bright and sunny and a fair-sized field turned up for the last day's cub-hunting. Two days later they would meet again to start the fox-hunting season, in full hunting uniform.

They went to Hungarton Osiers first. As Asher blew them into the covert he watched Merlin carefully. His heart sank when the young hound stood behind him for a while and then walked calmly into the undergrowth. *Enough of him,* he thought savagely and kicked his horse forward more sharply than was necessary.

They found in the osier beds and pushed the fox out across country. Asher blew the lilting notes of the "gone-away," as he trotted out of the covert to go after his hounds. They hunted slowly in the poor scenting conditions and Asher knew that the fox was getting farther and farther ahead. Stephen cantered up beside him, his horse sweating heavily.

"Fifteen couple, sir," he reported. "One short."

That no-good hound, Asher thought bitterly. *That's it. That's the end.* He saw Stephen swing his horse to go back for the missing Merlin and called out:

"Leave him, lad! Let him rot there if he wants to."

"Well I'll be," Stephen said, very quietly, and cantered on in Asher's wake.

But Merlin turned up of his own accord ten minutes later. The line had petered out at last and Asher had given the fox best. He was hacking across the fields towards the purple smudge of Hungarton Wood when he saw a lone hound trotting calmly across the pasture towards them. When Merlin joined in with the pack, Asher did not even look at him; he felt a deep sense of hurt, as though he had been let down by someone from whom he deserved better.

They arrived at Hungarton Wood and Asher blew hounds in. The sky was clear and blue and it was uncomfortably hot for men and beasts alike as Asher pushed his way into the dense wood.

He touched the horn and cheered them, his voice ringing out clear and thrilling in the still air.

"Yoi try! Yoi try-hy! Yoi rouse him there!"

He heard distant rustling and crackling as the hounds forced their way through the mass of briars and undergrowth.

"Yoi try-hy! Yoi, my beauties!"

He emerged from the thick of the wood into a clearing in which tall trees stood. He felt something wet on his cheek and wiped the back of his hand across his face—was surprised to see a double smear of blood on the white glove. He reined in and listened intently to the sounds all round him. The body of the pack seemed to have drawn through the wood, almost to the far side, without finding—but he knew the scent was poor and they must go on trying for a while. He gathered the reins up and was about to move on when a flash of color caught his eye just ahead—he froze into a statue-like immobility as Tag stepped delicately out of the undergrowth and stood looking full at him, one slim foreleg raised, black-tipped ears pricked, the flash of white showing vividly over his left eye.

Chapter Eleven

TAG WOKE FROM a dreamless sleep. Only his eyes opening showed that he was awake, for he did not move otherwise. He was lying curled on a couch of dead leaves in the heart of a bramble patch, his brush wrapped round him and over his sharp muzzle. He lay, blinking, for a while, then uncurled and stood up in one graceful movement. He stretched languidly, his nose pointed up to the sky, his hind-legs extending behind him, first one and then the other, his brush quivering with the muscular tension. When he had finished stretching he shook himself and trotted out of the bramble-patch towards the edge of the wood. Stars were still shining, powdered thickly over the sky, but the trees on the horizon towards the east were sharp-etched.

He drank from a puddle in the corner of a field near the covert, then trotted round the boundary of his territory, sniffing at occasional signs from other animals, and leaving scats of his own beside them to reiterate his claim. The sky was a high translucent azure as he trotted back into the wood to sleep again.

He was woken, some hours later, by sounds that were somehow familiar. He listened carefully, his ears moving, his nostrils wrinkling as he tested the air. Not particularly disturbed, he stood up, stretched again, and left his couch to go and investigate. Suddenly he stopped dead, and froze in an attitude of attention as the first hound's voice echoed through the woods. Memories flooded back to him as another hound, and then another, threw tongue. Tag slipped forward again, flitting through the dense growth like a golden shadow; every nerve in his body was tingling with a feeling of expectancy. More hounds' voices rang out, and then a different voice, clear and unmistakable, as Asher cheered his hounds:

"Yoi try-hy!"

With mounting excitement, Tag went forward at a lope towards the sound, expecting Merlin to be somewhere near. He heard the voice again, much closer, and then the sounds of Asher's passage through the undergrowth. He was totally unaware that he was in mortal danger—how could he know, after being brought up in a Hunt kennel? He was used to having hounds all round him, and even to bullying them. He had been safe then, for his natural fox-scent had been overlaid completely by the smells of Ruin and her litter: now, after seven months in the wild, there was nothing left of the kennel smells—only pure fox. Already, at the other side of the wood, hounds who had played with him through the lazy days of May were speaking to his line.

He ran past a group of hounds going the other way—their noses were down as they searched for scent and they failed to see him, even though he made no attempt to evade them. He slipped line an eel through a barrier of thorns and stepped out into a clearing to come face to face with Asher...

Tag felt no fear, only an intense curiosity. After holding the huntsman's keen gaze for the space of a deep breath, he blinked his slanted amber eyes and looked around the clearing, but there was no sign of

Merlin. Asher still had not moved: after a last speculative look, Tag turned and leaped into the undergrowth to go and search for his old companion.

A minute later, he found him. The young hound had wandered into the wood and was sitting on his haunches at the base of a huge sweet chestnut tree. When Tag appeared in front of him like an apparition he froze in disbelief—the next moment Tag leaped at him and was licking his face and neck and whimpering ecstatically. Something snapped in Merlin's brain: the restraint of seven months broke and disintegrated and he went raving mad—with a choking howl he leaped at Tag, knocked him off his feet, and began licking him madly, then leaped and whirled in crazy circles, while Tag pirouetted and panted around him. With the first excess of joy spent they became calmer, but still they rubbed against each other like cats, licking and whimpering.

On the other side of the wood, and drawing closer, the pack was hunting a line—Asher, strangely, was silent.

The idyll of their reunion was broken violently when a hound suddenly appeared only a few yards from them: it was Affable—the misnomer of all time, for she was a bad-tempered old dog, and a real fox-killer. Without a moment's hesitation she changed direction and hurled herself at Tag in deadly silence—Merlin saw the movement out of the corner of his eye and leaped sideways, startled. This movement saved Tag's life, for Merlin cannoned into the old hound, whose leap was deflected by just enough—Tag was knocked sprawling with a gash across one hip from the old dog's teeth. He got up, bewildered, and turned to face his attacker—she sprang at him again, and at last Tag realized that she meant murder. With a whisk of his brush he leaped to one side and ran for his life.

Merlin was puzzled—it seemed to him that Affable had barged in on his game, but when she went charging off on Tag's tail, throwing tongue, he naturally joined in the fun.

Still not very frightened, Tag was slipping along at a good speed, while not far behind old Affable hunted him with Merlin in tow. Soon hounds were running to Affable's excited baying and the chorus was growing. To Merlin the whole thing had suddenly become a delightful game—they were all playing "tag" and Tag was "it," or something like that. He ran with the body of the pack, throwing tongue joyously.

Asher, sitting tensely on his horse in the middle of the wood, knew that they were hunting Tag and was helpless; he could only wait and see what would happen. He heard the chorus swelling as the pack got closer to Tag and knew suddenly that the fox would have to break for open country. He kicked his horse forward so as to get with them.

While Tag ran ahead, Merlin was having the time of his life: he was in the van of the pack, flying along just behind Ardent, who had taken over the lead from Affable. He could tell from the strength of Tag's scent that his friend was only just in front . . .

Stephen saw the fox leave covert like a red arrow. Properly trained, he sat absolutely still while Tag scorched across the grass towards open country. Somewhere behind him someone started to holler but the sound was stifled at birth by a roar of "Silence, madam!" from Kendrick. Seconds later the pack burst out of covert in the fox's wake, and at the same moment Asher galloped out fifty yards farther down and swung across on a course that would unite him with his pack at the far side of the field. So accustomed was Stephen to the huntsman's quiet, taciturn manner that he was astonished when Asher galloped past him like the wind yelling, "Look at that, lad! Just look at that! Look who's leading 'em!" The next second he was flying the stake-and-bind into the next field. Stephen had not noticed the leading hound and could only follow on mystified.

Meanwhile, things were beginning to go better for Tag. Scenting conditions were terrible in the open and his superior speed—over a short distance—gave him a lead which was increasing steadily. Two fields behind, Merlin had forged into the lead and was hunting Tag's fast-fading line, owning it with his beautiful tenor baying.

"What a voice!" Asher exclaimed aloud. He had forgotten his distress at the idea of hunting Tag in his elation at the sight of Merlin suddenly catching on—and not only entering but taking the lead in bad conditions. Perhaps Asher's lack of concern for Tag was also due to his realization that the fox would get away—there was no chance of getting up to him now.

Tag had lost the last traces of his fear; it is characteristic of wild animals that they only experience fear when danger actually threatens—as soon as the danger is removed, they relax immediately. He loped along easily, catching his breath and looking over his shoulder from time to time to see where the hounds were.

Merlin could hardly hunt Tag's line, so faint had it become. He came to a hedge and forced his way through a gap: the scent died abruptly on the plough that lay beyond. He swung upwind, silent now that he could no longer own the line—Asher saw this and breathed a prayer of thanks for it showed that honesty was another of the hound's virtues. The pack spread out across the plough, heads down and sterns waving, unable to find the slightest trace of Tag's line. Asher gave them a minute, then popped over a post-and-rail into the plough and started to trot up the dead furrow. He took out his horn and blew a few short notes to lift the hounds' heads and carry them with him. They ran to his summons and preceded him along the headland. Merlin reached the hedge at the far corner first and Asher heard him whimper as he crashed through, then whimper again. "Yoi at 'im, Merlin! Hark 'ark 'ark to Merlin!" he cheered. The pack flew to its new leader and gave tongue in support as they picked up the faintest traces of scent.

Half a mile ahead Tag paused to drink from a cattle-trough, then leaped lightly up on to its rim; from this vantage point he looked out across the rolling country towards the distant line of Hungarton Wood. He could just see the tiny dots that were the hounds, as they struggled to follow his line across a field with bullocks in it. It had not been a conscious action of Tag's to run past the bullocks, but its result was the same: the line died completely on the foiled ground, and Asher asked the Master if he might call it off.

"Very well, Asher," Kendrick replied.

"Do you want to draw again, sir?"

The Master looked at his watch.

"No, they've had a hard day and there's no smell. We'll go home."

"Right, sir."

Asher touched his cap and turned back towards his hounds, who were sitting or lying in a loose-knit group, panting heavily. He put the horn to his lips and blew the long drawn-out "Going-home," letting it die slowly until it trembled into silence. Stephen appeared at his elbow.

"All on, sir," he said.

"Thank you, Stephen."

Asher walked his horse across the stubble to where Merlin stood—one of the few hounds still on his feet. He halted a couple of yards in front of the hound and sat there, looking down at him. Merlin looked back at him, a long steady gaze, and Asher saw that the cloud had gone from the hound's eyes—he looked deep, deep into them and felt something in him reach out and touch something deep in Merlin's brain.

"Merlin," he said softly. "Here then, Merlin."

For a moment he thought that nothing was going to happen, but then the white stern moved, just a fraction—then again, a definite wag this time. He felt a leap of exultation and called out in a ringing voice:

"Merlin! Here, son!"

And Merlin stepped forward gravely, stood up on his hind-legs and set his forepaws on Asher's foot, looking up at the huntsman steadily and unflinchingly. Asher leaned down and touched the hound lightly on his domed forehead, as though giving him his blessing. Merlin dropped on to all fours again and Asher moved forward to call the pack together and set off for home. He knew now that it was done: the miracle had happened.

Jogging home in a contented silence, Asher could hardly keep his eyes off Merlin—he was so alive now and showed an interest in everything. Asher looked at the easy swing of his stride and the perfect symmetry of his muscular little body; he remembered the way he had driven forward on the line, his honesty when it faltered and his beautiful bell-like voice. He was so full of happiness that he simply had to say something to somebody. He turned in the saddle and called back to Stephen:

"You just watch that hound go from now on!"

The whipper-in smiled back, affected by Asher's boyish grin and evident pleasure. Then he remembered what he had said in the pub only a few days before and felt acutely uncomfortable. *Why,* he thought, *he was right all along about that hound— he knew it all along.*

Chapter Twelve

NEITHER MERLIN NOR TAG looked back again after their fortuitous reunion. It is impossible, yet again, to say why. It was as though their meeting had given them the promise of more to come—as though they had realized suddenly that their separation was partial, rather than absolute. As though, now that they had met once, they both knew that it could happen again. And would.

When Asher included Merlin in his pack for the Opening Meet, he experienced a momentary qualm and found himself wondering whether the young hound might not revert to his former apathy. He shrugged it off, and hours later Merlin was forging to the front as they went away on the first official hunt of the season.

Watching the young hound as the days went by, Asher saw him begin to fulfil his early promise. Although he had wonderful qualities, he could still learn a lot about hunting from some of the old hounds, and this he began to do. On the other hand, he had something that no other hound in the pack possessed: he had an intimate and detailed knowledge of the ways of the fox, and combined with this was an uncanny understanding of how a fox's mind would work in any given situation.

At first Asher could not see how the young hound could possibly have done some of the things he had plainly seen him do—he could not understand how he could go into a vast covert and make his way unerringly to where a single fox would be lying, for example. It was only when Tod told him about some of the things he had seen when Merlin and Tag had lived together in the woods that Asher began to get a gleam of light. After thinking about it, he came to believe that the old man was on the right track with his theory that the two animals' personalities had somehow intermingled.

So Merlin went on improving, becoming steadier and more mature every day. Within a couple of months he had virtually become the leading hound in the pack—not absolutely, because when they were not hunting, the old dog-hounds held domination, and would allow no usurpers—but as soon as Asher blew them into covert, Merlin came into his own, and the huntsman came more and more to rely on him.

There was just one thing that Asher noticed: although it was Merlin who found most of the foxes, and Merlin who led the pack most of the time while they hunted their fox, he had never seen the young hound in any way involved in a kill. As soon as they ran from scent to view, Merlin seemed to lose interest and fall back, and it was the other hounds who killed the foxes.

Merlin and Tag met again half-way through January. It was a raw, wet day and Tag was dozing on his couch in Hungarton Wood when he heard distant and familiar sounds. He left the covert and trotted up to a vantage point a quarter of a mile away, from which he could plainly see the Hunt in the distance. Minutes later he saw a red-brown speck appear a couple of fields away, heading fast for the wood.

There is no explanation for what Tag did next, unless it be put down to some form of *joie-de-vivre*;

certainly it was not meant to draw hounds away
from his vixen, which is what it finally did. He leaped
forward and raced flat-out down the hill, on a
course which would intercept the path of the hunted
fox. He reached one end of the big pasture beside
the wood at the same moment as the other fox
entered it from the far side. Tag ran hard to try to
intercept it, but it ran into the wood yards ahead of
him. He plunged into the undergrowth and followed
the other fox into the heart of the wood, running on
its exact line. When the other finally swung off to
one side, looking for somewhere to hide, Tag ran on
and straight out of the wood on the far side. Feeling
strong and full of running he set his mask for the
distant horizon and went.

Asher saw the distant speck of the hunted fox as
it crossed the last field into Hungarton. Scent was
improving every minute and the hounds were
running well, with Merlin amongst the leaders all
the way. As they approached the wood, he turned in
the saddle and waved to Stephen, indicating that he
should go on round to the far side of the covert in
case the fox ran straight through. He saw the
whipper-in swerve away and looked back to his
hounds in time to see the leaders plunge into the
dark mass of the wood. He heard them hunting
through the covert as he cantered down a ride
towards the far side. He heard a momentary
hesitation and then a stronger cry than before, with
Merlin's voice easily identifiable. He checked his
horse, then pushed it on again when he heard the
change in the quality of the hounds' baying as they
ran out into the open.

As he emerged, he saw Stephen cantering down
the covert-side towards him.

"Did you see him?" Asher shouted.

"Yes, sir. It's him again!"

"Who?"

"That fox of yours—Merlin's pal!"

"Well I'll be—," said Asher.

The moment Merlin caught the first breath of Tag's scent, he knew who it was and threw himself forward with renewed zeal. Some of the older hounds tried to stick to the hunted fox, as was proper, but a combination of the certainty in Merlin's voice and the greater strength of Tag's scent decided the issue: the pack left the line of their original quarry and got on to Tag's.

A fresh fox always leaves a stronger scent, and the stronger the scent the louder and more certain is the baying of the hounds. Asher had heard this sudden surge of confidence in their cry and immediately suspected that they were on to a fresh fox, but he was quite unprepared for Stephen's report that it was Tag they were on to. It was hardly the time to worry about that, however—they had already run six or seven miles on the line of the first fox, and now there was a fresh, strong quarry ahead. Asher crammed his cap down on his head and settled in to ride.

Tag leaped and capered for sheer joy as he ran . . . the air was cold and invigorating and the turf felt springy beneath his feet. The following wind blew snatches of hound-music down to him, and from the medley of voices he could clearly distinguish Merlin's. There was no memory in his mind of when he had been hunted in Hungarton Wood—running for his life with the hounds only yards behind—but he remembered the game he had played afterwards, leading them on a wild goose chase across the fields, and now he was playing the same game again. Merlin, too, was playing the game, throwing himself into it with everything he

had. It was so like the times when they used to play
in the woods, when Tag would run ahead, trying
every trick in his possession to throw him off the
track, while Merlin would stick doggedly to the
scent, unravelling the puzzles that were set for him.
In those days, when at last he caught up with Tag,
there would be a joyful reunion—and this game that
they were playing now would end the same way, but
for one thing: the fact that the other forty-odd
hounds in the pack didn't feel quite the same way as
Merlin.

Over the first mile Tag drew ahead of the pack,
but after that he slowed down a little and they began
to gain. He slowed down on purpose—in fact at one
point he forgot the hounds completely and chased a
rabbit that got up under his feet, but without
success; it was not until he heard the hounds—quite
near by this time—that he ran on.

At the point where Tag had sprung to the side
and chased the rabbit, the pack checked. Their
momentum carried them thirty or forty yards on
before they began to spread out, noses down,
searching for the line. Asher cantered up to them on
his tired horse, rather glad of a short check. He left
them to make their own cast first—as does every
good huntsman—and watched them carefully. He
saw Actress suddenly swing, over on the right, and
heard her whimper. In a flash Merlin had run to her
and the next moment his joyous baying proclaimed
that they were on the line again. Asher looked back
to see Stephen just arriving, and a few blobs of
scarlet and black, three or four fields away. He
grinned as he urged his tired horse on again. *This'll
sort 'em out,* he thought.

After that first check, hounds settled down and
began to hunt steadily; it was not a strong scent, but

at least it was consistent, and for a little while Asher
had only to follow in the wake of the pack, for they
needed no help. As he cantered on, saving his horse
as much as he could, he became aware that a part of
his mind was worrying—he had a niggling feeling
somewhere that something was wrong...exasper-
ated, he forced it to the back of his mind and
switched his full attention to the pack in front of
him. *My goodness,* he thought, exultantly, *listen to
their music! Keep your brass bands and your
massed choirs—just let me listen to that*...the
chorus faltered, surged and faltered again, then
died. Asher saw the hounds spreading out as they
lost impetus, their noses down assiduously. He put
his horse at the hedge into the field in which they
had checked and slowed to a walk. Looking around,
he noticed cattle bunched in the far corner of the
field—almost certainly, they had galloped after the
running fox and foiled his line. Asher gave them a
chance to make their own cast, but he was fairly
certain that Tag had gone straight on, so after less
than half a minute he picked them up and began his
own cast. The moment he touched the horn and
called them they flew to him, such was their trust.
He took them at a fast trot round the far side of the
field, expecting them to pick up the line at any
moment—but, to his surprise, there was not a
whimper. When he had completed his circuit he
paused for a moment to think...He was distracted
momentarily by the arrival of the field—or what
was left of it—then he re-applied himself...*Where
did he go?* he asked himself, frowning, already the
hounds were looking up at him anxiously, for he
had taken them away from their cast in order to
execute his own—and when a huntsman does that,
he has to be right, or he will lose a little of his pack's
respect. He made up his mind. "Come along,
beauties," he called, "co-ope then!" He jumped into

the adjacent field and started to cast them back the
way they had come, but on a wider arc. At the last
moment—only yards before they reached their
original line—they hit it off again. As he galloped on
after them, Asher offered up a silent *thank you* to
his ancestor, the great Tom Smith, who had just got
him out of a lot of trouble...

By this time Tag was so far ahead that he could
no longer hear the hounds. He had been loping
along steadily for some time, and now he slowed to a
trot as he neared the brow of a hill. At the top he
turned and stood looking back over the valley
across which he had run: still no sign of the Hunt.
Tag sat down to wait.

Hounds were hunting steadily, and again Asher
found himself worrying...yet what could be
wrong? For the second time, he forced it to the back
of his mind. Scent was beginning to fail and he
reckoned that Tag must be almost ten minutes
ahead by this time. He knew there wasn't a chance of
catching him and had just decided to call them off at
the next check when something caught his eye. They
were approaching a hill, hunting quite slowly now,
and a red-brown speck was moving down the hill
towards them—moving fast...

"What the—" he exclaimed, and reined in
sharply. He turned to look for Stephen, but the
whipper-in was still some way behind, bringing on a
couple of hounds that had left the line to hunt a
hare. Asher stood up in his irons to get a better view
and stared towards the hillside, his eyes narrowed to
slits.

"I don't believe it," he muttered, and sat down
heavily in the saddle. "I *don't* believe it!"

Tag had the devil in him—the game had slowed

down to the point where it had become boring, so now he was going to liven it up a little...he ran down the hill with his brush streaming out behind him, straight towards the oncoming hounds.

It was Merlin who saw him, as the fox rocketed past only thirty yards away, going in the opposite direction. Because they were hunting a failing line, the hounds were concentrating hard on their noses and would possibly not have noticed a double-decker bus going by, but something made Merlin look up...with a whimper of excitement he swung round and went after Tag as hard as he could go.

From one field away, Asher watched as Tag flew past the laboring pack, holding his breath as he waited for them to see the young fox, but only one hound turned and sprinted after him. With an overwhelming sense of disbelief, Asher saw Tag turn and run back towards his old friend—saw the foxhound and the fox meet and whirl in an ecstasy of delight, capering and dancing in the middle of the field in which he stood like a statue, while the rest of the pack toiled on up the hill, away from them.

It didn't last for long...old Affable, who was well towards the rear, caught a whiff of Tag's new line, for it was being blown diagonally across the hillside by the east wind. She swung and spoke to it, breathing it in eagerly and giving tongue in a series of excited yelps. The rest of the pack turned and came back to her, and within seconds they were tearing back down the hill on a breast-high scent.

As Tag heard the chorus ring out, he licked Merlin's face once more, then turned and set off down the valley at top speed. Merlin went after him for fifty yards or so, then stopped suddenly and stood waiting for the rest of the pack. As they came up to him he turned and galloped forward at their head—and only now did he begin to give tongue.

As they disappeared over the hedge at the far side of the field, Asher pulled himself together and set off after them.

In the study that evening, Kendrick found the huntsman subdued. He himself was full of the day's sport, for it had been a memorable run, but Asher was withdrawn and said very little.

"What's the matter," Kendrick asked once, "sorry you didn't catch him?"

But Asher would not be drawn. In the end Kendrick dismissed him, half amused and half worried, for he enjoyed his sessions with Asher more than he would have admitted. Already, Asher's involvement with Merlin and Tag was creating complications in their easy friendship.

Walking slowly up the hill towards the kennels, Asher was still searching for the one elusive factor: the "wrongness" that had been worrying him all day—or, at least, ever since he realized that they were hunting Tag again. And try as he might, he could not pin it down and look at it.

He ate his supper and afterwards sat by the fire in a brooding silence—for Cathie knew better than to try to talk to him in this mood, and discreetly warned Jenny to keep off as well. When Tod came round, soon after ten, Cathie brought in his mug of soup and then went up to bed, leaving the two of them together in the parlor.

For a long time, while Tod supped noisily at his soup, Asher remained silent; not until the old man had finished and set the empty mug in the hearth did he speak.

"We hunted Tag again today," he said.

Tod belched and patted his stomach.

"I know," he said with a complacent grin.

Asher was startled out of his distraction.

"You know?"

"'Course I do," the old man muttered scornfully," and yer didn't catch him, neither, 'cos I saw him come home."

Asher had known, of course, that Tod spent much of his time watching Tag, but he had not realized that the old man was so closely involved and knew so much about the fox's movements. He fell silent again as he digested this, while Tod stared contentedly into the fire and sucked the last of the soup from his straggling moustache. The clock on the mantelpiece chimed out the half-hour and then the three-quarters before Asher finally made up his mind.

"I'm worried, Tod," he said at last.

"Ah," the old man replied, without any visible sign of interest.

"I'm worried about hunting Tag," he went on, "there's something…just not right about it, somehow—"

He broke off and looked up to see that Tod was laughing silently, his huge frame shaking, his old face fragmented into a hundred splinters of derision. Asher frowned.

"What's the matter?" he asked.

Tod drew a deep breath and controlled his laughter, shaking his head as he did so.

"I shouldn't worry about it if I was you," he wheezed, and wiped his watering eyes with the back of a huge hand. "Young Tag'll look after hisself, I reckon."

"You don't understand; it's not Tag I'm worried about."

"Then what *are* yer bothered about?"

"I don't know."

Tod shrugged, and Asher made an effort to control himself. He went on in a quieter voice:

"There's something peculiar starting up between those two devils, and it bothers me."

Tod tried hard, gazing deep into the huntsman's troubled eyes, but it was no use: he couldn't see anything to worry about—in fact, he reckoned Asher was making a lot of fuss about nothing. He spat expertly into the dying fire.

"Stop chauntering, boy," he said brusquely, "there's nothing wrong."

Asher felt angry and confused—the old man's curt dismissal of his plea for help rankled and he attacked without thinking:

"You'd change your mind pretty quick if we killed that precious fox of yours—"

"What!"

Tod reared up, staring at Asher, then let out a bellow of laughter that echoed through the house.

"Kill Tag!" he shouted, as though unable to credit his senses, and laughed again.

"There's only one hound'll ever best that one and you know as well as I do he'd no more kill him than fly."

"I've got thirty couple more that would—"

"Aye, and they'll never catch 'em. Mark my words, Asher Smith: yon's no ordinary fox. Yer may hunt him again and again, but yer'll never catch him—never!"

Chapter Thirteen

CATHIE WAS DOING her Sunday-afternoon stint in the garden, so when someone knocked at the door, Asher answered it himself. To his surprise it was Kendrick.

"Come in, sir," he offered, but Kendrick shook his head.

"No thanks, Ash, can't stop—look here, have you seen this?"

He held out a magazine, folded open for inspection. Asher saw a photograph of a fox, and the title of the accompanying article: "The Belstone Fox."

"Ah yes," he said, "I remember—that'll be Mr. Kearley, when he came down for the day—"

"But have you read it, man?"

"No, not yet—why?"

Kendrick was frowning, as though disturbed; he hesitated a few moments, then came out with it:

"Look, Ash, did you tell him about Tag? I mean, about him growing up in the kennels?"

"Of course not. Three years ago we agreed—"

"I know what we agreed. Are you *certain* you didn't let it slip out accidentally?"

"Yes, sir."

"Well, I don't know . . ." Kendrick shook his head and looked down at the magazine in his hand.

"What's the matter?" Asher asked.

"He gets pretty close to the truth, that's all."

"Well—" Asher shrugged, "He knows his stuff, doesn't he?"

"'Spose so..." Kendrick muttered, then he brightened up:

"Oh well—sorry I doubted you, Ash. I'd better get along."

He turned to go, then swung back and pushed the magazine at Asher.

"Here—you'd better read it," he said, grinning suddenly. "You're one of the principal characters."

*   *   *

The Hunt magazine, April 1966:

THE BELSTONE FOX:
A report by B. L. Kearley.

The annals of hunting are rich with accounts of the amazing cunning of the hunted fox. Some of the tricks with which they are credited border on the fantastic, while others are employed daily by such lesser animals as rabbits, for example. There is one common factor to all of them, however, and that is the readiness with which they are accepted as proof of the intelligence of the fox.

Now, I have contested this interpretation of the facts for many years, but the extraordinary case of the Belstone Fox has forced me to review at least some of my long-cherished beliefs. Although a painful process at the present moment, I believe that the outcome will prove beneficial, as must always be the case when long-held convictions in the field of animal behavior are shaken by new information. (Was it Konrad Lorenz who said that a good observer should relinquish one long-cherished theory every morning before breakfast, in order to maintain an open and inquiring mind?)

The Belstone is one of the less fashionable Midland Hunts. It is, however, one of the few remaining "Family packs." The Mastership was taken by Mr. J. M. Kendrick on the death of the ninth Earl of Belstone. In fact, the correct title of the hunt should be "Lord Belstone's Hounds," but it has become known simply as "The Belstone" through long usage.

Huntsman to the Belstone is Asher Smith. He is a member of the famous hunt family, and is a direct descendant of Tom Smith, of the Brocklesby— probably one of the greatest huntsmen of all time. Asher himself, at 55, has a high reputation as a hound-man, and Belstone hounds figure prominently in the awards at Peterborough.

THE LEGEND

Three seasons ago, towards the end of the cub-hunting period, a young dog-fox with a vivid white streak above his left eye gave hounds a short run from Hungarton Wood before scent gave out. This was the first known appearance of the now famous Belstone Fox. Later in the season they hunted him again, having changed on to him from a tired fox, and proceeded to chalk up one of the best runs of the season. Once again he gave them the slip, and the legend was born. Were it not for the clear identification mark on his mask, it would be logical to ascribe the exploits of this one fox to a dozen or so, but he has been seen too often and by too many people to doubt the legend any longer.

These are the facts: He was hunted three more times that season, once from Hungarton and twice from distant coverts. Two of these hunts were short and sharp, but the third was memorable, with a point of twelve miles and about seventeen as hounds ran. After a long report in *Hunting Today,* he acquired the sobriquet of "The Belstone Fox" and his fame began to spread beyond the boundaries of the Hunt.

From then until the present time, the legend has grown and is still growing. The hunt has received an increasing number of visitors from all over the country, who go there in the hope of a run from the Belstone Fox. This last season the Belstone entertained two Masters of Foxhounds from the United States, as well as a number of sportsmen from Europe. Even John Huston came from Ireland for a day and was lucky, finishing well up after a hard hunt.

All this is so much fact, and cannot be contested. But what startles me is the presence of certain implications inherent in the behavior of this remarkable fox.

Asher Smith has recounted to me, in great detail, most of the Belstone Fox's ploys. Many of them are normal procedure for an experienced fox, but some of them are indeed remarkable. On one occasion, for example, Smith clearly saw him running across the backs of a tightly-packed flock of sheep; when the sheep broke up and started to run, the fox maintained his place on the back of one of them while it ran for fifty yards or so, and then jumped to the ground, or was shaken off.

Another characteristic of this fox is his apparent familiarity with the appurtenances of what we in the country call "progress." He has, on many occasions, made a wide detour in order to run through the gardens in front of a row of houses, and twice has been seen to run into a house through an open back door, leaving via an open window at the front! This must sound like fiction, but the instances are well authenticated, and identification is fool-proof.

Another story, not quite so easy to verify, is that

he jumped up into the back of a slowly moving Mini-van and was driven away from the scene of the hunt. The driver did not notice him, unfortunately, but at least a dozen other people did; when someone told Asher Smith, who was still casting his hounds at the point where the line was broken, he flatly refused to believe the story, thinking that he was the butt of a joke in rather poor taste; but when the story was verified, later, he was forced to accept it.

But perhaps the most astounding of all the facts about this unique animal is one that may not be immediately apparent. When you consider the number of times per season that this fox is hunted, and when you then consider the unorthodox situations in which he is "found," you begin to wonder exactly *who* is finding *whom*. One or two examples will explain my point—and both, definitely, are true. The first occurred when hounds were drawing Burnetts Wood one morning in December, '65. They were in the process of drawing it blank when the field were startled to see a handsome dog-fox appear over the skyline and trot calmly past them—not more than fifty yards away—and into the covert. It was, of course, our friend. One minute later, hounds "found" him and an enjoyable hunt ensued.

The second example, which must surely be some sort of record, was when our fox actually turned up at the Meet. It happened at the village of Scarford in February of this year, when hounds were meeting on the green. About eighty people had turned up mounted, and a good number of foot- and car-followers as well, when someone noticed that the fox was sitting on a nearby wall, surveying the scene with great interest and evident enjoyment!

Now, the implication of these two occurrences, and of many others, is inescapable: it is that the Belstone Fox actually "finds" the hounds, rather than vice versa. In short, if they don't go looking for him, he goes out looking for them.

To be truthful, I cannot explain this phenomenon away. I must accept it without understanding it—a bitter pill for a so-called "expert." It is well known that hunted foxes often show signs of enjoying the "game" of being hunted, especially when on top of the situation, but to go out looking for the hounds... I am lost for words.

INTELLIGENCE?

The easy, anthropomorphic view is that this fox "enjoys" being hunted and so goes out looking for hounds for his own entertainment, but that is too facile. To talk of a fox "hoodwinking" hounds, or "out-thinking" them is to be guilty of a grave error, for a fox cannot "think" in a teleological manner—that is, like a human being, with an awareness of cause and effect and the ability to correlate unassociated data in a meaningful way. But, on the other hand, the facts are indisputable: this fox *does* go looking for hounds.

I can only believe that it has become some sort of private "game." What circumstances could possibly have combined to bring this about I cannot imagine, but I believe that this theory touches somewhere near the truth. Much of an animal's capacity for "cunning" and inventiveness is traceable to the urge to play and has little to do with intelligence—when that word is employed in its correct context. It is my belief that the Belstone Fox is no more intelligent than another fox of the same age; but I do believe that he has worked out, or stumbled upon, a highly ritualized "game" which he plays with the hounds. How he has managed to play this hazardous game so frequently without losing his life is just one more of the many questions that I cannot answer.

The final instalment of this "cliff-hanger" is by no means written. It will be interesting indeed to see how the situation develops pregnant as it is with possibilities. I can only say, in conclusion, that I hope that it is never my sad duty to write an obituary in these columns to the Belstone Fox. Good luck to him!

"Well, well," Asher murmured, "Kearley wasn't so far from the truth, at that."

He put the magazine down, staring thoughtfully out at the spring sunshine. He was still like that when Cathie came in, half an hour later, in a state of excitement.

"Just take a look at this, Asher," she exclaimed, and thrust a newspaper under his nose. "We're getting famous, all of a sudden!"

Asher grunted and started to read:

THE FOX THEY CANNOT KILL

Supporters of the Anti-blood-sports movement will be delighted to hear that one fox, at least, has turned the tables on its bloodthirsty pursuers.

Although it has been chased many times by the Belstone Hunt, the combined efforts of forty hounds and over a hundred huntsmen have failed to catch it. The fox is easily recognized by a white mark over its left eye, and it has become known as "The Belstone Fox" to huntsmen everywhere.

Hunt Master, 58-year-old John Kendrick, refused to comment when I telephoned him at his stately home near Cawsdon, Leicestershire. Huntsman A. Smith also refused to comment, presumably on orders from his employer, but Hunt member Mrs. Mary Stapleton, 29-year-old mother of three, was less reticent. "He really is a fantastic fox," she said, "and very popular with members of the Hunt." When asked whether she would like to see this beautiful animal torn to pieces by the hounds, she said, "Oh no, of course not. Anyway, they'll never catch him."

As though it were not enough to catch the attention of the national Press, the Belstone Fox may shortly move into folklore, for Doug Raven, the well-known folk singer, is at present writing "The Ballad of the Belstone Fox." "It will tell the story straight," he said last week, from his apartment in London's S.W.7. "I don't have any feelings one way or the other about fox-hunting—it's just a great idea for a song, that's all, with this crazy fox tying everybody in knots all over the countryside. It's like the Scarlet Pimpernel all over again."

With hunting in its close season until the autumn, the Belstone Fox has a few months in which to gather its strength and cunning for the next round in the battle. This newspaper wishes it the best of luck.

"Pop-singers..." Asher muttered disgustedly, shaking his head.

"But how about Mrs. Stapleton?" Cathie said, her eyes shining.

Asher looked up at her

"How about her?" he asked.

"Well..." Cathie was deflated immediately. "What will Mr. Kendrick say? Her talking to the newspapers, I mean."

Asher re-read Mrs. Stapleton's comments.

"There's no harm in what she says," he murmured, handing the newspaper back to Cathie.

"Well, anyway," she threw back, as she bustled out of the room again, "we're getting quite famous, and you can't say anything about that!"

"More's the pity," he muttered, when she had gone.

14th October, 1966   Bagdale Cottage,
                                      Cawsdon,
                                      Leicestershire.

Dear Jenny,

I expect you will be surprised to get this letter
from me. Your mother showed me the photograph
you sent last week, and I must say I was surprised
how sophisticated you looked in it. I think it is the
first time I've seen you without school clothes or
jeans.

I've just read what I wrote about being surprised
and it looks as though I'm being rude but you know
I'm not.

Well, I haven't any real reason for writing to you
except to say that if ever you feel like writing to me, I
would be very glad if you would I'm not very good at
writing letters myself, but I promise I will answer if
you write.

What day does your college break up? I hope it is
before the 18th because you promised you would
come to the Farmers' Dinner with me, remember?
                                      Love from
                                      Stephen.

"Well now," said Mrs. Sammells settling herself
comfortably in her seat, "tell us about your holiday,
love."

Cathie giggled; she was still a little patchy from a
bout of sunburn, but the fortnight in the cottage in
Devon had obviously done her a lot of good, for she
was effervescing with high spirits.

"Oh Norah, I must tell you—" Cathie said,
leaning forward in her chair, her eyes sparkling with
suppressed laughter: "It's Asher, you see—he had
such a *dreadful* time..."

"Oh dear—was he ill?" Mrs. Sammells asked,
radiating concern.

"Who, Asher? Good gracious no, he's never ill—

you know that. It was missing his hounds did it—"

"Did what?"

"Stop interrupting and I'll tell you. The first night we were there, about nine o'clock, he said to me: 'I'm going to sleep tonight, Cathie—I can hardly keep awake now.' That's exactly what he said, and I felt the same—you know what the air's like down there by the sea?"

Mrs. Sammells nodded encouragement.

"Well," Cathie went on, "we went to bed and I went out like a light, straight away—never woke up until past eight the next morning. And d'you know the first thing I saw when I woke up..."

Cathie was finding it difficult to control the laughter, which was bubbling dangerously near the surface—she contained it with an effort, and went on:

"There was Asher sitting in a chair by the window fully-dressed and shaved and trying to read a book—and you know how often Asher reads books..."

Mrs. Sammells nodded eagerly.

"So I asked him what the matter was—ooh, he was in such a mood, you've no idea! He nearly snapped my head off—"

"What *had* happened?" Norah demanded, for she felt that Cathie was making the story over-long.

"Well, he'd fallen asleep straight off, just like I did—and he stayed asleep for about half an hour, he reckons. Then he woke up—with a jump, like—certain that something was wrong. He lay there worrying about it for hours until he realized it was because he couldn't hear his darling hounds and, do you know, he never shut his eyes again that night, nor the next night!"

The two women exploded with laughter, giggling like a pair of hysterical schoolgirls over a naughty story, then Cathie tried to pull herself together:

"But the funniest part is—" she gasped, "he never

got *one* proper night's sleep, and d'you know what he had to do in the end?"

"No?" wheezed Mrs. Sammells, wiping the tears from her eyes with the back of a plump hand.

"He couldn't stand lying in bed, so he had to sit downstairs in an armchair, wide-awake all night, and—"

"Oh my goodness!"

"And then every time we went out anywhere in the daytime, he'd start falling asleep all over the place—he nodded off in a pub one day and dropped his beer on the floor!"

Mrs. Sammells screamed with laughter, her eyes screwed shut, holding her ample sides and rocking to and fro...

"I hear you tore it up a bit, on holiday," Frank Sammells remarked breezily, the following day. Asher looked across at him, his eyes narrowed.

"What d'you mean?" he asked suspiciously.

"Well..." the kennelman was smiling innocently: "you know—staying up all night, burning the candle at both ends... is that why you looked so—"

"There's a carcass just come in," Asher snapped, "Perhaps you'd care to go and get cracking on it?"

"Right, boss," Frank said, still grinning, as he strolled off towards the flesh-hovel. "And it was worth it, an' all!" he told himself gleefully, as his nostrils caught the first penetrating whiff of decomposing cow.

Hunting Report: *Hunting Today*, 12 November, 1966:

BELSTONE

We are happy to report that "The Belstone Fox" has turned up again. During cub-hunting we had no

positive sighting, although there were a few
"possibles." Last Saturday, however, after the
opening meet at Cawsdon, our old friend was
clearly seen going away from Burrows Wood. The
ensuing hunt was almost as good as any he has given
us in previous years, and while it was not as fast as
some, it was certainly farther as hounds ran, than
most. In moderate scenting conditions, hounds
stuck to their job admirably, across the difficult
country between Cawsdon and Selby Gorse. Once
over the turnpike, they ran on across the grass and
must have been quite close behind our friend when
he ran into Harberton village. Asher Smith did well
to hit the line off on the north side of the village; it
was an inspired cast, for he had swung back upwind,
contrary to all expectations. Hounds ran strongly
across the vale as scent improved, and the odds on
"catching him this time," came down to 3-to-1 when
he was viewed climbing Grimthorpe Hill with a
muddied brush. Here, however, he gave us the slip
yet again, for the old badger setts were unaccounta-
bly unstopped, and he got to ground. A point of
only seven miles, but a good thirteen as hounds ran;
and good news, indeed that the Belstone Fox is with
us for yet another season.

"Tod?" Asher said.

The old man turned, halfway down the path to
the front gate; Asher clearly saw the inquiring lift of
a bushy eyebrow in the moonlight.

"Just a matter of interest," Asher went on, "*did*
you stop the Grimthorpe badger setts?"

"'Course I did—yer told me to, didn't yer?"

"Then how come he got to ground there?"

The old man hesitated, as though uncertain for
the moment how to reply.

"Well..." he said, at last, "you know them owd

badgers, Ash—they'll pull anything out, they will."

"I know *one* old badger that would, anyway," Asher said softly.

Tod glanced up furtively, but he could not read the huntsman's expression in the dim light. He chuckled silently, then turned and shambled away into the night.

28th Jan., '67   Harkham Teachers'
                                  Training College,
                                  Fulborough Avenue,
                                  Hull, Yorks.

Dearest Steve,

Thank you both for your letters; please forgive me for not replying sooner—I've been up to my eyes getting everything ready for my first classes, which start next week. I'm very nervous, but I think I'll be able to cope all right.

Yes, I had a wonderful evening, too—thank you so much for taking me and for being so sweet.

Stop running yourself down! You write lovely letters. They always make me happy so they must be good, and anyway my English grammar is appalling, so stop worrying.

Must stop now as I am very tired and I have to be "alert and intelligent" tomorrow, if that's possible! Write again soon, won't you?

    Fond love,
      Jenny.

5th Feb.   Kennels.

My dear Jenny,

Enclosed is a little something to help you with that evening dress. I know it will cost more, but this is all I can manage at the moment. I hope you have a nice time at the ball. Peter sounds like a nice young man. The hounds are mostly well, and so is your mother.

> Your loving
>> Father.

P.S. Don't forget you must not tell your mother about this little present. It is a secret between you and me.

15th Feb., 1967   Eastwell House,
                                   Blatchford,
                                   Kent.

Dear Stephen Durno,

As you may have read last week in *Hunting Today*, George Gillatt has decided to retire at the end of the current season, due to persistent bad health, following a fall; we shall therefore be looking for a replacement in the very near future. The committee have asked me to write to you and inquire whether you might be persuaded to take over as huntsman in May. We note that this is your seventh season with the Belstone and feel that you might possibly be ready to make a move. Your reply, naturally, will be treated in the strictest confidence, and should you signify your interest in the idea, we shall then make a formal request for your services.

> We would be grateful for an early reply,
>> Yours sincerely,
>> F. G. Arnold
>> (Hon. Sec., Medvale Hunt)

"But . . . why ask me?" Cathie wondered. Stephen shrugged.

"I don't know," he said. "Who else can I ask?"

"Well..."

Her voice trailed off as she realized that there was, in fact, no one else... but what could she say?

"Stephen, I don't know..." she said, shaking her head anxiously, "I mean, what do you *want* to do?"

"I just don't know," he muttered, staring gloomily into the mug of tea she had given him.

"Poor Stephen," Cathie whispered, not realizing that she had said it aloud.

"Look," Stephen said suddenly," I've been here nearly seven years, now, and I reckon I was ready to hunt hounds after three, or maybe four. It's *time* I was hunting my own pack—so why don't I just write back and say yes?"

"The Medvale's a good Hunt," Cathie added.

"Exactly," Stephen said, "The Medvale's a good pack to be huntsman to—"

He fell silent again, brooding over his tea.

"So why don't you go?" Cathie persisted—then noticed that the young man had flushed and was trying to hide his confusion. She felt her pulse quicken as the first glimmerings of a thought slipped unbidden into her mind.

"Tell me," she said.

"Don't you know?" Stephen muttered—and suddenly the knowledge was there: complete, as though she had known for a long time.

"Jenny," she whispered.

He nodded, but kept his face averted from her. She held herself still as she fought to control a sudden emotional upheaval: she was astonished to discover that she was on the verge of tears, but whether for joy or sorrow she could not tell. Suddenly, the tension was released and she could speak at last:

"I'm so happy," she said.

*   *   *

28th June, '67   Hotel Los Alamos,
                                  Torremolinos,

Dear Asher—hope you like this postcard. This is a terrible place. I wish I'd never let them talk me into it. It's so hot all I can do is drink water all day. How is Challoner's hock? And how about that draft from the Brocklesby, any more news? Did they fix the roof in the stables? Blast this stupid bit of paper, there's no more room. I'll probably be back earlier than expected, so watch it.

                                  John Kendrick.

10th July, 1968   Harkham Teachers'
                                  Training College,
                                  Fulborough Avenue,
                                  Hull, Yorks.

Dearest Steve,

Only another week,—I can't believe it!

I do hope you're not still upset about Peter; I've already told you that that's all over and done with, and I shan't mention it again. Really, you should try not to get upset so easily, Steve—you're such a sweet person, apart from these flare-ups. Why not make a resolution not to have any more, as from right now? Then we'll be able to have another marvelous summer, like last year.

Try not to worry too much about father, I'm sure you imagine most of it—after all, why on earth should he disapprove of "us?" He always speaks so well of you to other people. If it's still bad when I get home, I'll have a talk with him, but I'm sure it's your awful sensitivity again!

I'll tell you all my news when I see you. Don't forget: 19.30 hrs. at Grantham. Longing to see you.

                    Fondest love,

                              Jenny.

Stephen looked at his watch, for the fortieth time that afternoon, and didn't even register the time it showed, for his mind was already reaching ahead to Jenny's return, that night...

"Stephen!"

He jumped as Asher's voice cut through the daydream like a whiplash, and turned guiltily to see the huntsman standing over by one of the grass-yards.

"Come here, please."

Stephen hurried across, wondering what he had done to displease him. Before he had arrived, Asher was pointing to the far corner of the small paddock.

"Look at that!" he snapped. Stephen looked.

"What d'you see?" Asher went on, inexorably.

"Well..." *the remainder of the puppies—they look all right to me. I wonder... Oh—that one on its own, over there...*

"Yes, that's the one," Asher said, in a dangerously mild voice.

"It's not well," Stephen said, lamely.

"Congratulations."

The young man flushed with anger, stung by Asher's sarcasm—but he managed to control himself. He stood up a little straighter.

"I'm sorry, sir," he said stiffly.

"I'm sure you are."

Stephen waited for a few seconds, in case Asher had anything more to say, then he turned and started to walk away.

"Stephen."

The huntsman's voice had lost its edge of ice—Stephen turned.

"Do you know why I was angry?"

"Yes, sir."

"Why?"

"Because I didn't notice that that puppy was off color," he said clearly.

"And why is it important?"

"Because it should have been isolated and treated straight away."

"Right. So what went wrong?"

Stephen shrugged.

"I don't know, sir," he said. "I just didn't notice it, that's all."

Asher looked at him for a long time: his face was impassive, but his eyes were cold—then, he nodded curtly and walked away. Stephen stood motionless, feeling angry and confused at the same moment.

"You're getting old and mean," he said to the huntsman's receding back, "why don't you give up and let a young man take over?"

Excerpt from "Preview of the season," *Hunting Today,* 24th October, 1969:

". . . In the rest of the Midlands there is little change. The Belstone are lucky to have Asher Smith for yet another season. In spite of rumors that he would be retiring, Asher shows no sign of wear and remains one of the very finest hound-men in the country today. Whipping-in will be Stephen Durno, who has been with them for more than nine years. It is no secret that he has been offered the post of huntsman to some very good packs over the last few years, and it is greatly to his credit that he has remained loyal to Asher Smith. When that great huntsman finally retires, there could be no more worthy successor than young Durno. While with the Belstone, I could hardly omit some reference to the grand old Belstone Fox, who gave them some really rattling runs last winter, and is now—we trust—getting into shape for yet another season's fun and games. Incidentally, this incredible animal must now be at least seven years old, which—for a fox—is knocking on a bit. It will be interesting, this season, to see whether there are any signs of slowing up on his part. For myself, I hope not—if ever any fox deserved a peaceful old age..."

Chapter Fourteen

"YOI TRY-HY! Yoi try rouse 'im there!"

Asher's voice sang through the stillness of the wood, frightening roosting wood-pigeons out of the trees with a clatter of wings. The hounds were spreading out, pushing through the thick wet undergrowth, questing for the first taint of fox. At the corner of the covert the field were waiting in silence when a sudden high-pitched yelping from the middle of the wood set hearts beating faster—but not Asher's.

"Tester!" he growled, as though he could warn the young hound by telepathy to get off the line of that rabbit and on with his job—he could tell immediately by the pitch of a hound's voice whether the scent was rabbit, deer or fox.

The hounds reached the up-wind end of the wood, turned and started drawing down again, combing every square yard for a trace of their quarry. Asher blew two quick encouraging notes on his horn, then two more, and cheered them again, trying to lift their spirits with his voice, to keep them trying, trying.

"It's blank," a scarlet-coated visitor remarked to his neighbor, outside the covert, "I wonder where—"

"Be quiet!" Kendrick snapped, without even looking—then added, under his breath:

"What do you know about it, anyway?"

The back of his neck gradually returned to its normal hue, and the visitor breathed again. There was a time when Kendrick had been unable to maintain discipline in this manner—swiftly and decisively—but fifteen seasons' experience as Master had given him an authority that near-millionaire status in the business world had never brought. He shifted in the saddle and patted his horse's neck absent-mindedly as he listened to the huntsman's voice ringing out in the depths of the wood:

"Yoi try! Yoi try wind 'im there!"

Again, Asher blew the quick, encouraging notes on his horn, telling his hounds that he was still with them and asking them to persevere...persevere ...then the short hairs on the back of his neck prickled as the damp November morning was pierced by a view-holler from the far side of the wood—a thin, eerie yell that set horses sidling and champing at the bit and started a pair of jays screaming in panic. The air was suddenly vibrant as men crammed their silk hats farther down on their heads, shortening their reins and easing nearer the front so as to get a good start when they went away...Kendrick held up one white-gloved hand and controlled his mount with the other—he could feel its heart, beating with excitement, through the thick leather of his top-boots.

When Asher burst out of the wood, Stephen was standing like a statue at the far side of the field with his horse's head pointing in the direction the fox had taken. Asher cantered towards him, calling the pack to him with urgently-repeated notes on his horn. He looked back halfway across the field and saw that more than half the pack were already behind him, while the remainder were pouring out of the covert at a dozen different points.

"Was it him?" He shouted as he galloped up to Stephen.

"No, sir."

"Never mind," Asher said, as he put his horse at the hedge into the next field, where hounds had already hit off the line.

They ran strongly for almost a mile before a ploughed field checked their progress. Asher pulled up and gave his horse a blow while the hounds began to spread out, noses down and sterns waving, searching for the elusive scent. As always, his eyes searched for and found Merlin... the old hound was a little heavier and more scarred, his manner more that of the elder statesman, otherwise he was the same hound who had first spoken joyously to the line of the Belstone Fox six long years before... a whimper snatched Asher out of his reverie—then another.

"Hark 'ark 'ark to Merlin! Yoi at 'im old dog!" he cheered, as the rest of the pack flew to their leader and confirmed the line. Asher trotted forward down an open furrow and kept quiet as they hunted slowly across the cold-scenting plough. His heart beat a little faster with sheer joy as he watched old Merlin leading them, working the faint trail every foot of the way with absolute honesty—only speaking when he was certain of the line, and casting again the moment he was unsure of it. At last they came to the end of the plough: Merlin wormed through the stake-and-bind fence and flung himself forward across the grass. Asher heard the sudden surge in the pack's music and knew that the scent was lying better on the old pasture. He glanced back in time to see Stephen jumping out of the plough behind him and Kendrick holding the field in check, over on the far side—then he switched his attention back to his hounds as he let the big thoroughbred stride on across the ridge-and-furrow. Merlin was still leading them but Asher noticed that the old hound was going with a hurried stride, as though hard pressed. He urged his horse on so as to see better and drew level with the pack just as a young hound named Trimbush suddenly burst forward and started to overhaul the leader. Merlin seemed not to notice until the youngster had come up to his shoulder— for a dozen strides he tried to accelerate and keep the lead, but Trimbush held his own and then started to creep ahead as the old hound put everything into a final effort. Asher watched with bated breath, knowing what was coming, yet willing it not to happen...

In his prime, Merlin had always led the way when scent was poor, because of his incredible skill: when scent was good—cancelling the advantage of his ability—he had still been fast enough to stay at the front, and so he had become accustomed to being always in the lead. Now that age had slowed him down, he could still lead them in difficult conditions, but as soon as there was a strong scent, the younger and faster hounds began to overtake him. Asher's heart had bled for the old hound, seeing him strive desperately to regain the lead, but he had dropped farther and farther back. As soon as the young hounds lost the scent, Merlin would come up with them, blowing like a grampus, and put his wonderful nose to work: soon he had found the line and was forging ahead again—but seconds later the same young hounds would creep up to his shoulder, up to his head, and finally past him, leaving him to toil along behind once again. After bearing it stoically for a while, Merlin was beginning to resent this state of affairs, and for some time now Asher had been waiting for the old hound's patience to snap. He watched carefully as Trimbush began to

inch ahead...then his heart sank as Merlin
suddenly turned on the young hound and bit him
savagely on the side of the shoulder—Trimbush
yelped with pain and surprise and dropped back
immediately.

"Oh no," Asher said clearly, watching helplessly
as another young hound, and then another, drew
level with Merlin, only to be met with the same
treatment. After a few more unsuccessful attempts,
the eager young hounds curbed their enthusiasm
and kept their place behind Merlin.

Asher had seen the whole performance and
cursed bitterly—for a jealous old hound can soon
ruin the confidence and initiative of the young
entry, and he knew that if it went on he would have
to start leaving Merlin at home. He knew, too, that
this would break the old hound's heart, and dreaded
the time when he might have to make a decision.

The rain had started just before they packed up
and now it was falling in a steady drizzle. The
pattering of the hounds' feet on the tarmac was
always louder on a wet road and Asher heard it now,
a whispering, rushing sound, like distant rapids. It
would be dark soon—already the color was seeping
out of the landscape and he could see lights in the
windows of a distant farmhouse. He shifted in the
saddle to ease the ache in his legs, but nothing he
could do would lessen the pain in the small of his
back—the legacy of a fall ten years before. He
thought fleetingly of the hot bath he would have and
fire he would sit by, then shrugged it off with an
effort—the kennels were still four miles away. He
tried to blank out the cold rain, the discomfort and
the aches by thinking...about anything so long as it
took his mind off his present situation. *Had a good
day,* he thought, with a glow of pleasure. *They
hunted well, must have been nearly a hundred out—*

quite a few visitors, too. Twice the number we used to have. I bet they were hoping the Belstone Fox'd give 'em a run—I suppose I was, too, come to that. He doesn't come looking for us the way he used to. Must be getting old, like the rest of us... He looked down at his favorite, trotting steadily and apparently tirelessly in his usual position, by Asher's right stirrup. "Merlin," he said softly—the old dog-hound looked up at him and waved his stern in reply. *Six years,* he thought. *Six years*... He looked down at Merlin again.

"I'll tell you what," he said aloud, "this'll be your last season, old dog..." *and probably mine as well. Kendrick can't go on much longer, either. We're all getting old together... even Cathie's going gray. It's their turn next—Stephen and Jenny, and the rest of the young entry*...

He looked down at the close-packed hounds and singled out the young ones, just entered: Dasher and Dauntless, Whimsey, Little Harlequin, Prophet and Priestess, Artful, Trimbush, Marksman and Madrigal...a fine, promising bunch of youngsters. He saw their strength and their *joie-de-vivre*, even after a hard day's hunting, and remembered Merlin at his best...

He lived over old runs then, in the days when Merlin had led the pack with effortless pride, until at last the lights of the distant kennels shone reflected in vertical blurs along the wet road, ahead of them.

Later that evening, when the hounds were fed and put away, Asher went up to the big house. Kendrick, too, seemed to have age on his mind on this wet, miserable evening; snug and secure in the warmth of the study, they were both thinking of the many times they had sat like this, sipping their drinks and discussing the day's sport. In a sudden flash of insight, Asher realized that he would miss these evenings badly, when he retired...and Kendrick must have had the same thought, for he leaned forward suddenly and said: "Let's go on doing this when we've both put our boots away, Ash. It's become so much a habit I don't think I'd know how to stop it."

"I'd like that," Asher replied.

"We'll sit here, exactly as we are tonight, and we'll talk about what we would have done if we'd been hunting hounds. Ash, I believe we'll make a splendid pair of drawing-room fox-hunters, don't you?"

Asher smiled:

"I believe we do already," he said.

Kendrick laughed delightedly.

Later, they talked about Tag. Although he had become known throughout the country as "The Belstone Fox," Asher still thought of him—and spoke of him—simply as Tag.

"You going to try and catch him this season?" Kendrick asked, casually. Asher was taken by surprise.

"But...I always do try, don't I?"

Kendrick looked at him owlishly, over his reading-glasses.

"I don't know," he said. "Do you?"

Asher was scandalized:

"Of course I do!"

"Are you sure you've *really* tried to catch him?"

"Yes, of course."

"Are you absolutely certain," Kendrick went on, inexorably, "that you've never helped him, just the tiniest bit?"

Asher thought carefully and shook his head.

"I don't think so," he said at last. "Have I?"

Kendrick chuckled and sat back in his armchair.

"I think so," he said.

"But when?"

"Well... how about the time you marked him to ground in the Stoneworks Earth? Why didn't you send for the terriers and dig him out?"

"They were a long way off, as I remember."

"Come off it, Ash—they weren't that far away— any other fox I reckon you'd have had out of there. And then how about the time they couldn't find his line down in Cantwell's Water Meadows? You saw him lying up in that willow, didn't you—hm?"

Again Asher was caught off balance.

"How the devil did you know that?" he asked, indignantly.

Kendrick laughed, pleased by the success of his thrust.

"Ah..." he said mysteriously, "I've got spies everywhere."

"Tod," Asher muttered, "I'll wring his scrawny—"

"Now then, Ash, you'll do no such thing—he wasn't telling stories out of school: he only told me because I was interested in his precious fox. I still am, come to that."

Yet Asher was strangely disturbed to find that his secret was out. He remembered the strange sense of ill-omen that he had experienced, six years earlier, when first he learned about the "game"... remembered the intuitive feeling that it was wrong somehow, to let it go on; then his gradual acceptance, and finally his active participation, which went as far as bending the rules quite considerably, when he thought it necessary. And now they all came flooding back again: the nagging feelings of doubt and guilt, the formless fears, and— strangest of all—the creeping sensation of being on the rails . . . of following a path already determined for him, and of being powerless to turn away, to either side . . .

"What's the matter, Steve?" Jenny asked, for the third or fourth time.

"Does it show that much?" he asked. "I thought I'd been doing pretty well."

"I don't know what gave you that idea," she remarked, tartly.

It hadn't been much of an evening for Jenny—at first she had decided that Stephen must be tired, after the first full day's hunting of the season, but later she had begun to doubt this. Now they were sitting in his car—a careworn but reliable old Ford—listening to the rain drumming on the roof. After a long silence, Stephen sighed deeply, then took two cigarettes from a packet in the glove-compartment and put them both in his mouth. Jenny looked across at his profile, lit momentarily by the flame of the lighter: his face had a stillness tonight which she had never seen before—he was usually so animated. He handed her one of the cigarettes and drew deeply on the other, not looking at her.

"Steve—" she began, but he forestalled her.

"Your father tore me off a strip today," he said unemotionally, then he chuckled—more like his usual self—"In fact that's the understatement of the year. To be honest, he tore me to pieces."

Jenny was shocked, and felt a sudden rush of sympathy for the obviously chastened young man.

"But, what for?" she asked.

"Oh . . . quite a few things really. It's the longest speech I've ever heard out of him, and he didn't waste a single word."

Jenny knew how Asher was when he was really

angry—the quiet voice cutting like a knife and the terrible strength of the man's control over himself: more daunting than any display of temper could ever be. She leaned forward and laid a hand gently on Stephen's forearm, but he seemed not to notice. He was staring out through the windscreen at the darkness of the trees behind the kennels.

"I think I must have deserved a lot of it," he said—more to himself, as though she were not there—"but I don't think I deserved all of it."

Jenny squeezed his arm, sympathetically.

"I think he hates getting old," she said.

Stephen felt a sudden spasm of fear and glanced up at her quickly—*could she have guessed?* he wondered—but he saw only gentleness in her expression and looked away again, relieved.

Over the years, as his feelings for Jenny deepened, he had fought to hide from her both his secret ambition and his increasing impatience to realize it—for he knew how close was the relationship between Asher and Jenny, and was unsure of her reaction, should she ever find out. Apart from himself, only Cathie knew of his delicate situation— some of it Stephen told her, and the rest she had guessed—but he knew intuitively that the knowledge was safe with her, for Cathie would never consciously do anything to jeopardize the progress of the romance she desired so much. She never bothered to analyze her own motives, although it was easy to see that with Jenny in love—and later, married—Asher's close relationship with his daughter would virtually disappear, and Cathie would then have him all to herself.

A sudden flurry of rain against the windows pulled Stephen back to the present, and all at once he became acutely aware of Jenny's hand on his arm: he looked down at it, then covered it with his own and looked up into her eyes. Jenny knew, suddenly, that he was going to say something, and though she knew what it was—her heart quickened within her, but she gave no sign.

"Jenny..."

Come on, she was thinking, *get it over with— you've been wanting to say it for a long time*...she squeezed his arm again, to encourage him, and saw him decide to say it—she held her breath...

"Jenny, I want to tell you something..."

Yes?

"In spite of how it may appear, I'm very fond of your father—"

???

"and I have the greatest respect for him."

When he saw that she was obviously waiting for more, he added, lamely, "That's all."

For a few seconds he couldn't read her expression—it seemed to be a mixture of emotions. Then she started to laugh, as though some restraint had just snapped. Stephen was puzzled. "Have I said something funny?" he asked, in a hurt voice. Jenny laughed even more, her head thrown back, then—to his astonishment—she flung her arms round his neck and kissed him full on the mouth, with the laughter still bubbling out of her parted lips.

By the time Stephen took Jenny home, Asher had returned from his session with Kendrick; he had bathed and eaten his supper, and was now sitting by the fire in his dressing-gown, staring into the flames. He hardly looked up when Jenny came in and merely offered a perfunctory cheek for her to kiss. Later when Cathie got up and went out to the kitchen to prepare their bedtime hot drinks, Jenny put her book down quickly and went over to Asher.

She knelt on the floor in front of him, with her hands on his knees, and looked up into his deep, hooded eyes . . . she was searching for the twin to her own need—she knew that it had to be there, somewhere: the need to get back to that plane of loving intimacy on which they had always lived, and shared their most secret thoughts—but now she saw only reflected firelight and the tip of an overwhelming sadness. Asher stirred uneasily, embarrassed by her gaze.

"What d'you want, my love?" he asked.

"Oh, Daddy—"

She squeezed his bony knees, impulsively.

"What's wrong?" she implored.

"Why should anything be wrong?" he countered, gently but firmly evading the question.

"I don't know," she said, "but something is—why won't you tell me?"

Asher looked away from her and back into the fire: his face was almost without expression, but Jenny could see the deep lines that bit downwards from either side of his mouth.

"Why are you unhappy?" she whispered.

He shook his head slightly, and frowned.

"Is it anything to do with me?" she insisted.

At this he turned and looked full into her eyes.

"No, of course it isn't," he said distinctly, "why d'you ask?"

She shrugged.

"I just thought it might be," she said.

Asher was still staring at her with a strange intensity—suddenly he took both her hands in his own and held them tightly, then smiled.

"No . . ." he murmured, "not you, my love. You least of all."

"Then tell me."

"Just hound-worries, that's all."

"Are you sure, Daddy? Is that the truth?"

He smiled again and raised his sardonic eyebrows.

"Of course it is," he said.

Then Cathie came in with the mugs of chocolate and Jenny went back to her sofa, more or less satisfied. While she lounged back with a magazine and sipped her hot drink, Cathie was watching her—discreetly, of course—from the other side of the room. No matter how she tried, Cathie could not get used to the change in Jenny: the schoolgirl who had gone away to college had come back so very much a woman: so quick and full of life; so sure, it seemed, of everything. Looking at Jenny now, Cathie could see Asher in her—in her dark, controlled quickness and her startling, direct gaze. Because she had come back so changed Cathie was a little afraid of her...she had noticed the same reaction in Stephen, too—and she smiled unconsciously as she remembered the young man's confusion when he brought Jenny home from the station, at the end of her last term. Cathie picked up her knitting and went on with her thoughts: *Such a nice young man, and so handsome, too*... Once or twice she had started to discuss with Asher the possibility that Stephen and Jenny might one day get married: she had been startled, and later hurt, by the vehemence with which he had objected to what was only a day-dream of hers...

"What makes you think they're even considering it?" he had demanded angrily, the first time she raised the subject.

"Nothing at all," she had replied hurriedly. "It was me considering it, not them."

"Well, don't go putting ideas into their heads, Cathie."

"Of course not. Why ever should I?"

"I don't know," he had muttered, "you might have your reasons."

That had ended the discussion abruptly, and now Cathie never mentioned the subject.

Jenny finished her drink first and went up to bed, feeling happier for having got through to her father—which is how she saw it, although Asher might not necessarily have agreed.

After she had gone there was a long silence. Asher picked up a copy of *Horse and Hound* and tried to read it, but his attention lapsed after a while and he went back to staring into the embers of the dying fire.

Cathie came out of her own private dreams and looked across at Asher: he was still sitting upright and motionless, looking for all the world like a pagan god, carved out of dark wood ... suddenly Cathie remembered something:

"Asher," she said.

He neither replied nor gave any indication that he had even heard her.

"Asher!" she repeated, trying to control her exasperation.

"Yes?" he replied at last, still not looking at her.

Cathie put her sewing down on the floor—her face flushed as the blood ran to her head.

"Listen to me, Asher, I want to tell you something important."

"I'm listening."

"It's about Jenny—"

At the mention of Jenny's name, he seemed to come to life, for he turned quickly and looked at her, for the first time.

"Well?" he said.

"It's something Norah Sammells told me, the other day. I simply refused to believe it at first, but—d'you know?—it's true, what she said ..."

"Get on with it, Cathie."

"Our Jenny—" Cathie pronounced, leaning forward and speaking slowly for dramatic effect— "is an ANTI."

"A what?"

"An Anti—"

But still Asher looked blank. Cathie sighed.

"She's against hunting," she explained finally, and waited for Asher's reaction.

It was not long coming: his eyes opened wide and all at once she had his undivided attention.

"Against fox-hunting?" he echoed, incredulously.

"Against all kinds of hunting, actually."

After a long pause, Asher started to laugh... almost imperceptibly at first, but with gathering momentum, he laughed at—well, he didn't know quite what it was that was so damn funny all of a sudden, but *something* was, or he wouldn't be laughing like that...

And when at last it was over he was almost his old self again. Even if only for the moment, the depression that had set in at the sight of Merlin's jealousy towards the young hounds had vanished like a bad dream.

Later that night, long after Asher and Cathie had gone to bed, the rain finally died away and Tod set off for Hungarton Wood in the fitful moonlight. He was still there shortly before dawn, and was beginning to worry about Tag's absence—for all the world like an anxious mother whose sixteen-year-old daughter is late back from her first party; but when at last the first birds were chirruping sleepily, Tag came home. The old man tensed as he saw the dim shadow drifting across the meadow towards the wood, then relaxed as the shadow resolved itself into the delicate outline of a fox...

Tod was standing at the edge of a clearing, and as Tag crossed the open space his sensitive nose caught a faint trace of the old man's familiar smell. He stopped, with one slim foreleg raised, and looked directly at Tod, from less than ten paces away...

"Hallo, son," the old man said, gently.

A pointed ear flickered, but otherwise Tag did not move: he was not afraid—merely curious to see whether his benefactor had brought a gift, as he so often did. Tod chuckled silently and fumbled in one of the deep pockets of his overcoat—Tag detected the movement and walked forward a couple of paces, his nostrils wrinkling eagerly as he tried to identify what was coming... and suddenly Tod got it clear of the pocket and Tag knew—in one glorious lungful of certainty—that it was a rabbit. His mouth opened in a smile of pleasure and his brush twitched with suppressed excitement. He watched as the old man laid the rabbit down on the damp bed of leaves, then straightened up again and took two steps back. Without any hesitation, Tag walked to the rabbit and picked it up, carefully, as though it were fragile. He looked up once more—Tod saw the dawn sky and the tracery of branches reflected for a moment in the slanted amber eyes—then turned and trotted away through the undergrowth, his head held high as the limp shape of the rabbit swung from his jaws.

Tod stared after the fox for a long time after he had disappeared towards the center of the wood; then, at last, he turned and began slowly to make his own way home.

Chapter Fifteen

THERE CAME A point when Asher's suspicion that the covert might be empty became an absolute certainty. Regretfully, he blew the first long notes calling the hounds to him, and walked his horse out into the open. He could just hear Stephen's voice on the far side of the wood:

"Go on leave it! Go on leave it!"

The huntsman positioned himself some thirty yards from the edge, still calling hounds with the horn. Within two minutes the whole pack were clustered round him, some of them bleeding from ugly cuts and scratches. Kendrick rode over and walked his horse carefully through the hounds to Asher's side.

"That's a surprise," he said.

"Aye, it is—I thought he'd be there."

"Perhaps he's decided to retire, after all."

"Not him, sir—he's probably laughing at us all, this very minute."

Kendrick shrugged, then said:

"Well... looks like the Osier Beds, then."

"Very well, sir."

Asher moved forward in the middle of his pack, like a scarlet-sailed galleon surrounded by a school of black-and-tan dolphins. With the field following a hundred yards behind, the Hunt moved off towards the next covert. It was a short ride across the side of the hill to the Osier Beds in the valley, and Asher was just jogging along over the grass when something caught his eye—he looked up the hill to his left and pulled his horse round violently at what he saw: Tag was sitting on the skyline looking down at the Hunt, and Asher could almost see the expression of mirth on the old fox's sardonic mask.

"Well I'll be—" Asher muttered, staring at the distant figure. Suddenly everyone had seen the spectator and a variety of shouts and hollers set the hounds looking around excitedly. Asher made up his mind:

"All right, my lad," he said grimly, "now we'll really find out what you're made of."

He turned and galloped forward up the hill, blowing the lilting call of the "gone-away:" the hounds streamed after him joyfully, although still unaware of the cause of the commotion, for they had not seen the fox. Asher saw Tag turn with a flirt of his brush and scoot over the skyline. He looked at the heavy sky, felt the air blowing cold against his cheek and saw that the woods on the distant horizon were a deep gray-brown...

"I think you've miscalculated this time, my old friend," he said to the invisible Tag, "but I hope not."

Suddenly he heard Merlin's full-blooded voice as the old dog-hound found the well-loved scent, and moments later the crashing chorus of the whole pack as they settled to the line and fairly flew across the top of the hill.

Tag was feeling good. Although no longer young, he was in good shape and the cold November air was invigorating. He had given the hounds two runs during October, but they had been shorter and less energetic than usual; now he felt full of running and set off across open country at top speed.

The private game that had developed between him and Merlin was a delight that had never palled for either of them. It was their only contact, and they enjoyed it. After a good hunt, in which the two old friends pitted their wits against each other, life seemed more colorful for both of them—the game seemed to lend zest to the everyday routine. As far as both of them were concerned, the other hounds might just as well not be there—it was their private affair, and no one else was allowed in. But at last something was happening which could upset the balance of the whole situation: age was beginning to affect them both, and the rest of the hounds were no longer a factor which could be blithely ignored.

He must be losing his senses, Asher thought, *he's running dead up wind. They'll have him in five minutes at this rate* . . . but he should have had more faith for the next moment the pack's cry faltered and ceased. He rode up to them and watched while they spread out, casting forward, into the wind. Out of long habit, he kept an eye on Merlin and was not surprised to see the old dog-hound casting back, on his own. Seconds later Merlin had the line again and the rest of the pack flew to his support when he spoke. Tag appeared to have stopped, turned and run back on his tracks, then to have made off at an angle to his previous line. The pack's speed had lessened fractionally now that they were running down wind, and Merlin was able to stay in the lead, although not without effort.

Asher put his horse at a rough hedge: halfway over he saw the glint of water in the dyke on the far side and felt the animal make an extra effort in mid-air—they just made the bank with a scramble and the horse picked itself up and galloped on while Asher sorted out his reins and felt for his stirrups. *There'll be some wet shirts there,* he thought gleefully, his eyes already ahead, looking for the blur of the flying pack. Thirty seconds later the field arrived at the same fence: Kendrick just cleared it, and so did the two men who jumped beside him, but after that came a series of accidents with horses dropping short and tumbling into the dyke; riders who were approaching the fence saw legs and hats flying—most of them thought better of it and hauled off to the right or the left to look for an easier route, but some crammed on anyway, and a few of these made it, too. In the end, apart from two loose horses, about thirty riders were left in the first flight, while the rest were doing their best to get in touch again after making a detour round the big fence.

Tag reached the bottom of the slope, still going strongly. Ahead of him lay Scalby Vale—a line of big black fences to cross before reaching the Yellborough Brook. He set his mask for the distant mass of Rowlands Wood, and ran...

Asher felt a twinge of anxiety when he breasted the hill and saw the pack streaming out across the Vale—as a young man his heart had lifted at the very thought of galloping at the big fences, but now he was older and sat more loosely in the saddle.

Behind him, as more and more people cleared the brow of the hill and saw the Vale ahead, there was a medley of reactions: Kendrick muttered then took hold of his good old gray and sent him on. Stephen said "Hah!" at the sight, and smiled, showing his white teeth. Men who had travelled a hundred miles that morning for the chance of hunting the Belstone Fox crammed their silk hats down and thanked Providence. The local doctor—an Irishman who hunted three days a week—looked to left and right

for possible casualties, determined to get ahead of
them and so avoid being detained. A good-looking
woman on a chestnut was looking anxiously over
her shoulder for a glimpse of her twelve-year-old
daughter and wondering whether she ought to wait
for her—she was looking in the wrong direction, for
the child was three fields ahead, her trace-clipped
pony skimming over the ground like a swallow,
going over, through, or even under every obstacle.

Half a mile farther on, another big fence caused
more trouble. The galloping doctor took it neck-
and-neck with another "regular," who turned in his
saddle and looked back as a riderless horse
overtook them, with reins and stirrup irons flying.

"I say, Tom," he shouted, "who's that back
there?"

The doctor turned and saw a pair of legs sticking
up out of the ditch.

"It's Bill Hodson," he remarked, equably.

"Shouldn't we go back and see if he's all right?"

"Ah sure," the doctor protested, "he's as fit as a
fiddle—didn't I check him over less than a week
ago?"

The thunder of hooves, the rush and crackle as
they flew the fences, the biting wind in their faces—
this is what it was all about for most of them. As
Jorrocks said: "The himage of war without its guilt
and only five and twenty per cent of its danger . . ."

But more than twenty-five per cent for Tag, who
was beginning to tire. Halfway across the Vale he
came to a line of ploughed fields; the wet clay stuck
to his paws and balled up until he was running with
heavy clogs of mud, which weighed him down.
When he reached the grass again his legs felt leaden
and there was a searing pain in his chest. With his
coat bedraggled and filthy and his brush dragging
the ground, it was a very different fox from the one

that had set off across the Vale, *corazon arriba*.

The cry of the hounds seemed to swell as they gained on their quarry. Merlin had battled gamely to keep the lead but the going had beaten him—the young hounds had inched past him and he had been too stretched to snap at them—first Marksman and Dasher, then Prophet, Harlequin and Dauntless, the young hopefuls on whom the future of the pack depended, fast and strong, throwing tongue to the breast-high scent...while Merlin, halfway back through the pack now, struggled gamely to keep on terms and would struggle till the end—for that was his nature.

Tag saw the muddy, turbulent water of the Yellborough, hesitated for a second, then leaped in. He turned his nose downstream and swam. The water was bitterly cold and a delicious numbness began to creep into the extremities of his limbs and spread upwards like a balm, but a gust of wind brought the sudden blood-music of the hounds and he was galvanized into action again: he started to climb up the far bank, struggling to gain a foothold on the crumbling earth—suddenly it gave way beneath his feet and he was plunged backwards into the icy water. Again he tried, slowly and painfully crawling up the steep bank—and this time he made it. When he ran on there was no feeling in his legs, his back was arched and his ears flattened—this was no game; not any longer. Tag was fighting for his life and time was running out on him.

Asher's heart sank as he saw the leading hounds leaping for the far bank of the brook and knew that he would have to jump it, for the nearest footbridge was nearly a mile upstream. He was tempted to pull up and look for an easy place, but he knew that to do so would be to lose all the impulsion and forward momentum that he so desperately needed. Fifty yards out he took a pull, then sat down to ride, not hurrying the big bay but keeping a good long stride. He saw the long ears flicker forward and stick there, felt the horse's speed increase as though it were being pulled towards the brook by a giant magnet, caught a glimpse of the swirling water even as the powerful hind-legs gathered beneath him and exploded them forwards and upwards . . . he experienced a sensation of hanging in mid-air, then felt the wind of his passage rushing past his face as the bank came up to meet him—the shock of his landing merged into an awful lurching and sliding motion and he hit the ground and rolled clear, already relieved that he was not hurt. He got to his feet in one movement, still holding the reins, and turned to see his horse fighting to gain the top of the bank, its forelegs buckled beneath its chest while its hind-legs thrashed and dug for purchase in the soft bank. A last heave and scramble and it stood before him, trembling and gasping from the effort. Asher patted its lathered neck before swinging up into the saddle and urging it forward again, his eyes sweeping the landscape for his hounds. He saw them to his left: they had lost the line and cast downstream, picking it up again a hundred yards along, and now they were running as strongly as before. Even as he watched, he saw old Merlin being overhauled again by the young hounds.

A movement caught his eye and he turned in time to see Stephen jump the brook in text-book style, then swing towards him.

"You all right, sir?" the whipper-in asked as he cantered up.

"Oh yes," Asher replied briskly, already urging his horse forward in the wake of the pack. As soon as it was cantering on, he turned and shouted:

"Stick with me for the moment!"

He saw Stephen wave a hand in acknowledgment, then looked ahead again to where hounds were running. He heard snatches of their music, swelling and becoming more certain as they made ground on the fast-tiring Tag. Asher successfully negotiated a rough hedge and heard Stephen follow him over, a couple of lengths behind. As always, he was hardly aware of the horse beneath him—his mind and all of his senses were focussed two fields ahead, where his hounds were running—and in this way he was almost running with them, breathing in the strengthening scent as they overhauled their quarry, while leaving his body far behind to bring the horse on—then he saw something, up ahead, and felt the first slow heave of fear, deep in his guts . . . six or seven fields in front of them, the grass-covered ridge of a railway embankment cut a clean line across the countryside, and the hounds were heading straight for it. Suddenly he came to life:

"Get over there!" he yelled at the whipper-in, waving violently towards the distant railway line, where it curved in towards them. "Get there and stop anything that's coming—for heaven's sake, hurry!" And even as he shouted breathlessly at Stephen, he was driving his own mount on, his arms and legs flailing at the exhausted horse as it galloped its best—but a Pegasus would have been too slow for Asher that day, for he could see his hounds already less than two fields from the embankment, and running like driven snow . . .

Tag was sinking . . . he heard the exultant note in the pack's voice and knew it was for him. He was barely able to move his legs, and his lungs were on fire: there was a singing in his ears and his vision was blurred. Something loomed up ahead, like a mountain—with painful slowness he toiled up the steep slope, and as he reached the top, hounds ran into the field that he had just left...

Asher saw the train first, but only just—for, moments later, Stephen saw it, too. After the first frozen seconds, Asher went berserk: he screamed at his horse and lashed it with a heavy whip, while deep in his entrails the fear was heaving and coiling...for he knew beyond all argument that neither he nor Stephen had a chance of getting there in time to stop it, or even slow it down.

Tag turned and ran slowly down the track, between the rails—every atom of will and strength concentrated on to the job of making his legs go on working. Ahead of him, a long way down the line, was a rapidly growing shape, but he saw nothing— nothing except the procession of sleepers as they crawled past him and the iron rails on each side. The hounds streamed across the field towards the embankment, the young entry again in the lead, with Merlin ploughing along towards the rear. Tag fought on, and was suddenly aware of a vibrating that grew and became a distant thundering somewhere ahead of him...the hounds poured up the steep bank in an irresistible flood—Dasher, leading them, swung left and galloped on down the track, with the fox's scent strong in his nostrils ...Tag looked up and saw the dark mass looming up and thundering at him—obeying blind instinct he flung himself to one side, using the last dregs of his strength, and rolled helplessly down the bank as the train roared past and ploughed through the leading hounds at seventy miles an hour, scattering them like confetti and leaving them broken and bleeding in its wake...

* * *

Asher saw them run up the embankment—seconds later the train slashed past and his heart tumbled over and over as he went on yelling at his horse, willing it to get there faster. A post-and-rail stood in front of him and he flung the tired beast at it desperately—it rose but was off-balance and hit the top rail hard. Asher felt it going and threw himself clear: he heard the agonizing *crump* behind him as the horse fell, but already he was on his feet and running like a madman towards the embankment, gasping in his distress, then clambering up the grassed slope in a frenzy...

It was like a battlefield...

There seemed to be corpses everywhere, lying broken and limp, like dolls mutilated and then thrown away. Asher stood, his chest heaving, looking around him. His hands were clenching and unclenching at his side and tears were running down his face. He walked to the first one and looked down at the mangled ruin: it was Dasher. He went on to the next, and the next... Prophet, and bright, loving little Harlequin, now twisted and bloody. Then Priestess and Whimsy, and a third-season hound, Talisman. He heard something and swung round, then heard it again: a bubbling moan. He leaped across the tracks and plunged down to where Marksman lay—his back broken and blood trickling from his mouth. Asher stopped, frozen where he half-stood, half-crouched, staring down. He stood up, crying like a child, and clambered wearily up to the top again. He could see the rest of the pack clustered together on the side of the embankment, aimless and whimpering. He knew that he should go to them and call them to him, but, for the moment, he could not. He stood there dumbly, shaking uncontrollably, a man without

direction. He heard Stephen's voice from behind
him saying "Oh, no...oh, no..." and moments
later felt a hand on his shoulder. He turned and saw
the young man's face, pale and haggard, and heard
him ask: "Are you all right, Asher?" but the words
meant nothing...Suddenly he lurched forward and
flung the whip away from him, violently.

"I'll get him!" he screamed. "I'll get his rotten
hide!"

Stephen helped him carry the corpses and lay
them out in a row, at the bottom of the bank. Then,
at last, Asher went to the rest of his hounds and
spoke to them and soothed them. His eyes registered
that Merlin was not amongst them, but it really
didn't matter. When Stephen returned with Asher's
horse, the huntsman seemed to be normal again,
until he turned to Stephen and gripped his arm
hard, staring into his face with piercing gray eyes:

"I'm going to kill him for this, Stephen," he
whispered.

"Yes, sir," the whipper-in replied, not knowing
what else to say.

Merlin had not been hit by the train because he
was too old to stay in the lead on a good scenting
day. The hounds that were killed were the pick of
the young entry: the future leaders. The train
thundered past only seconds before Merlin would
have reached the rails—he tumbled over backwards
in his terror, but as soon as the train had gone he
recovered himself and carried on down the track,
questing for Tag's scent.

The impact of the speeding train had carried the
leading hounds yards along the line in the opposite
direction, so Merlin never even saw them. In his
tenacity of purpose, he simply went on doing what
he had been doing before the train came. He picked

up Tag's line where the fox had leaped to avoid the train and tumbled down the bank; he forged ahead, throwing tongue, and never even noticed that he was on his own.

He followed the trail for another half a mile and found Tag just inside the edge of a spinney. The fox was lying on his side, breathing noisily. As Merlin came up to him, whimpering eagerly, Tag tried to rise, but fell back. The old hound stood over his friend, licking him and whining anxiously. After five minutes Tag still had not moved, so Merlin got down beside him with his forelegs stretched out in front, watching carefully for any movement.

Darkness fell and still Tag did not move. Merlin lay in the same position, waiting ... and at last the fox seemed to revive. He sat up in one convulsive heave and shook his head. Merlin stood in front of him, his tail waving, whimpering slightly. Tag stood up and staggered sideways, almost falling but just saving himself, then stood with his legs apart, trembling violently, his breath rasping in his throat. Still Merlin waited for the joyful welcome, the romping and tail-chasing ... he could not understand what was wrong with Tag; in his dedication to their private game, the tragedy had passed over his head, and he had no way of knowing that for Tag the game had turned into a nightmare in which he had almost lost his life.

Poor Merlin, standing perplexed, his tail beginning to droop, his forehead wrinkled, full of pleasure at the reunion with his old companion ... while Tag fought for enough to stand up, his body racked with pain, his lungs burning, dizzy, sick and trembling uncontrollably. After a little while he moved forward a few steps, walking straight past Merlin. The old hound watched, uncomprehendingly, as Tag halted and stood swaying; then he turned and went after him and stood a little to one side, watching closely for some sign of recognition—but Tag stood, motionless but for his trembling, with his head hanging almost to the ground, his mouth pulled back in a rictus of pain. Suddenly a whimper of desperation escaped from Merlin: he plunged forward again and started to lick Tag's pain-racked face. This time the fox did react: with a wailing snarl he slashed at Merlin with his teeth. The old hound stepped back, aghast, his tail half-moving, but Tag attacked again: this time he lunged at Merlin and bit him on the cheek, leaving no further doubts about his feelings. Merlin turned and ran a few strides, then stopped and looked back, the blood already dripping from the gash on his cheek, but Tag was not looking. The old hound whined softly and still Tag would not look. At last he turned away and started to walk, slowly, away from the friend of his lifetime. After a mile or so he lifted his head and looked around him in the darkness, then set off at a steady trot in the direction of the kennels.

Almost two hours later he was still trotting at the same unhurrying pace along a deserted road. Suddenly he lifted his head as he heard a distant sound—a sudden burst of barking that subsided immediately—and knew that he was nearly home.

I cannot claim that he was looking forward to getting home, or that he badly needed the warmth and friendship of Asher's company after losing his greatest friend—I cannot, because that would be expressing an animal's feelings in human terms. Yet—how else can I describe the confusion of emotions in the old hound's dim consciousness? Dumb misery...the aching of stiff joints...a fierce yearning for home, and—above all else— the soft voice and gentle hand of the man he loved with all his animal being. He felt a sudden stirring of pleasure as the kennel lights appeared over the brow of the hill, and quickened his stride.

Asher sat in his chair, wrapped in a dressing-gown, brooding. He stared into the fire and ignored the hot drink at his side. Cathie had been obliged almost to force him to change out of his hunting clothes; he had picked at his meal and now he sat staring into the fire. He had not said one word since entering the house—Cathie had heard of the tragedy from Frank Sammells and had warned Jenny not to disturb him.

When Asher heard the faint whining from outside the kennels, he got up and went silently out into the darkness. He opened the side-door and saw Merlin standing outside looking up at him, his tail waving slowly. The old dog-hound was waiting for Asher to say his name, as he always did, so that he could walk forward and greet the huntsman—instead, Asher stared down at him with cold, indifferent eyes. Merlin's tail drooped and he lowered his head a little, but he held the huntsman's gaze without flinching. After a long silence, Asher turned and walked away across the yard. He opened the door into the Draw-yard and turned: seeing the old hound standing where he had left him, still waiting for an invitation, he said "Come on," in a cold voice. Merlin walked forward obediently and through the inner door. Asher put him into the lodging-room without looking at him and without speaking to him again. When the huntsman had gone, the old hound climbed up on to the bench and lay down on the straw. He put his nose down on to his forelegs, his eyes wide open in the darkness, and started to grieve.

Asher was still slumped in his chair staring into space when Tod arrived, soon after ten o'clock.

Cathie had gone to bed and Jenny was out, so the old man let himself in and walked through the silent house to the parlor. When Asher saw him, he jumped slightly, as though startled, then looked away again and said nothing; Tod shuffled over to his usual chair and sat down awkwardly.

For a long time the old man waited for the huntsman to speak, for he could think of nothing to say. He sat dumbly, glancing up at intervals from beneath dense eyebrows and mumbling under his breath—but Asher remained silent. After ten minutes or so, Tod was feeling acutely uncomfortable. A couple of times he cleared his throat nervously, as though about to speak, but nothing came of it. He was about to get up and leave when Asher spoke, at last:

"I've got to kill that fox, Tod," he said quietly.

The old man was suddenly still and alert—like a wild animal, waiting tensely to be attacked again...

"I'm going to kill him," Asher said sharply, looking at him now.

Tod struggled to understand what Asher was saying, but for the moment it was too enormous—all he could see was the misery that swam deep in the huntsman's gray eyes. He groped for words, yearning to comfort.

"But . . . it was an accident," he said at last. "No one's to blame. It was an accident."

"*I'm* to blame," Asher said, quickly and fiercely.

Tod shook his head, as though trying to shake his thoughts free of cobwebs.

"Yer not to blame, lad," he said.

"Yes I am!" Asher shouted, violently. "They were playing a game, those two—all those years they were playing a game, and I played it, too. You know I could have killed Tag, once if not twice, don't you?"

The old man nodded. Asher went on:

"Well, it was wrong! It went against Nature, and that's why it's gone bad on us—all of us. Now I'm going to put it right."

There was a silence in the room, while both men looked inward at their own feelings. When Tod spoke again, minutes later, his voice was sad:

"Yer sound like a man who's made up his mind and ain't going to change it again—not for nothing or nobody."

Asher nodded, his eyes still fixed on the floor. "That's right," he whispered.

Tod shook his head and stood up, moving as though his body had suddenly become unbearably heavy. He stood motionless for a long time, looking down at Asher—his weathered old face pulled this way and that by conflicting emotions: of love, and pity, and grief...

"Yer going wrong, Asher," he said at last, "and yer can't see it, more's the pity. That's bitterness yer feeling, and nothing'll go right for yer as long as it's that that's driving yer. Ye'll find that out in time."

Chapter Sixteen

ASHER COULD NOT fight off the overwhelming sensations of guilt that surrounded him, paralyzing his ability both to think and to act. He had never experienced anything remotely like it before—had always felt himself to be master of both his actions and, in a wider sense, his destiny as well... yet now, his efforts to throw off this creeping paralysis had about them something of the feeling of an insect's frenzied attempts to escape from a jam-jar.

Asher's malaise affected everybody, to a greater or lesser degree. In the kennels, the daily routine went on unaltered, but there was a tension in the air that was all but tangible, at times. The hounds reacted noticeably to the atmosphere in the kennels: pack-discipline began to deteriorate and sporadic fighting was liable to break out at any time of the day or night. Under these conditions, nervous hounds became terrified; confident hounds became anxious; gay hounds became melancholy; idle hounds became restless; and—worst of all—surly hounds became actually dangerous, as Frank Sammells discovered when old Warrior's yellow fangs clicked shut, inches deep in his left buttock. And through it all, Asher continued to go around in a morose silence, only speaking when it became absolutely necessary. In the evenings, the house had all the gaiety and bustle of a morgue—Cathie hardly dared open her mouth, while Jenny gave up after the first night and kept out of the house altogether when Asher was in it.

But it was Merlin who seemed to suffer more than anyone else. Rejected first by his one great animal-friend, and then by the man he worshipped, the old dog-hound seemed to slip back towards what he had once been, many years before: a solitary figure, silent and withdrawn, standing quietly a little to one side of anything that was going on...

Kendrick waited, with all the patience he could muster, for Asher to come and talk to him... after three days had gone by, he gave up. He was half aware of what was wrong with Asher, and put the huntsman's behavior down to his grief at the loss of the hounds. Like Cathie, he felt that the situation would resolve itself best if left alone, while interference might possibly do more harm than good—meanwhile, they would be hunting again in two days' time and, surely to God, if anything could shake Asher out of his peculiar frame of mind, that would...

On the morning of the fifth day after the accident, hounds met at Billford. Asher was tense and preoccupied with the possibility of finding Tag. They drew Waldron's Thorns and found almost immediately, but as soon as Asher had ascertained that it was not the Belstone Fox, he continued with only half his attention. Hounds were running well and were on to a "traveller"—a fox caught away from his home territory, courting a vixen in strange country. Such foxes usually head for home in a straight line and often give a very good run. While Asher half-watched his hounds, the other half of his mind was calculating their probable route and assessing the chance of finding Tag somewhere along the way.

He was riding Challoner, a strongly-built bay and his most reliable horse. He could rely on the big gelding to the extent of merely pointing him at a fence and leaving the rest to him: this enabled him to concentrate on his pack and was a most valuable asset.

Asher saw the hounds crossing a wide dyke and turned away to where he knew there was a bridge, with sheep-hurdles to jump on to the bridge and off it again. As he cantered diagonally across the big field towards the bridge, he was still wondering where he could search for Tag. He saw that Challoner was going in the right direction and—as usual—left it to him. The big bay approached the bridge at a steady gallop and an angle of forty-five degrees. He saw his stride extended and took off, clearing the first set of hurdles nicely, while Asher looked away into the distance, where his hounds were running—next moment, Challoner struck the edge of the bridge a glancing blow and plunged with sickening force into the dyke. Asher was aware of the bank rushing up to meet him—there was a jarring crash and immediate oblivion.

Asher regained consciousness in the ambulance. After X-rays and a careful examination, a doctor pronounced him undamaged, but warned him that he would feel the effects of concussion for a day or two, and on no account should he work, or ride, or exert himself in any way at all for a period of at least two weeks.

The following evening, Asher was summoned to present himself in Kendrick's study at six o'clock sharp. He knocked on the door at two minutes to six and was invited to enter. By one minute past, Kendrick was in full spate:

"...Goodness sake, man, I don't know what's come over you—you must have turned into a raving lunatic or something."

He turned and glared at Asher—then his expression changed to one of concern as he noticed how pale the huntsman was:

"Er...look," he mumbled, "why don't you sit down, Ash?"

"I'd rather stand, thank you, sir," Asher replied.

Kendrick roared, pounding the desk with his fist, "Sit down when you're well told!"

He glared in silence as Asher sat down in an upright chair, white-faced but impassive—to all outward appearances, at any rate.

"Right—now..." Kendrick growled, trying to remember the next thing he wanted to say.

"Oh yes, that's it—poor old Challoner..."

He stepped out from behind the massive desk and started pacing up and down the center of the room, his hands clasped behind his back, his eyes fixed on the floor, moving with his characteristic controlled violence.

"Look, Ash—" he started, frowning fiercely, "that's a bloody good horse you've crocked—and I'll tell you something: he might be found again for next season and he might not. He nearly ripped one foot off and his legs are all knocked to hell—"

He fought valiantly for a moment or two against his volatile temper, then succumbed for the third or fourth time:

"What came over you!" he bellowed, still stamping up and down the room. "And not only that, but everything else as well—and to think I used to admire your control...hah!"

He slumped back into his swivel-chair and stared gloomily at the huntsman, drumming his stubby fingers on the leather desktop. At last he sighed, loudly.

"All right, Ash," he said, "that'll do for the

fatherly chat bit—now let's have a good row and clear the air."

Asher had to smile, in spite of himself—Kendrick saw it and grinned back at him, suddenly and irresistibly. Both men relaxed a little.

Ten minutes later, the last barriers of reserve had tumbled and the two men were back on their old footing again—and after a further half an hour, Asher was ready to tell Kendrick about the obsession that had almost killed him, the day before:

"It's to do with those hounds—" Asher began, finding it difficult and feeling his way slowly—"the ones that were killed, I mean. You see—"

"Oh, look here, Ash," Kendrick broke in, "we were all upset about that—and after all, they were *my* hounds, weren't they? But that doesn't mean—"

"Now hold hard a moment," Asher broke in, "there's a great deal more to it than that."

"Sorry, Ash," Kendrick murmured, apologetically.

The huntsman frowned as he tried to pick up the dropped threads—at last he shook his head in disgust.

"It boils down to this," he said, "I've got to kill the Belstone Fox."

Kendrick was frowning, as though puzzled.

"According to you, you've been trying to do that for the past six years without any success."

"But, don't you see?" Asher said, intensely. "I've really got to kill him now."

"Hold on, Ash—I don't think we see eye to eye over this. As far as I'm concerned, it was an accident—an unfortunate one, but an accident for all that—and I'm not going to have you running a private vendetta against the Belstone Fox, at the expense of—"

"Just a minute, I don't—"

"That's pure revenge," Kendrick exclaimed, his voice rising sharply, "I'm surprised at—"

Asher blazed suddenly, unable to take any more—Kendrick blinked twice and remained silent. Asher got up from his chair and went across to stand directly in front of his employer.

"Just listen, please," he implored. "You haven't begun to understand yet—"

Kendrick listened.

"Now look," Asher explained, "I've learnt a bit about how foxes work over the last forty years, and I'll tell you one thing I know: if a hunted fox accidentally discovers a way of throwing hounds off his scent, he'll use that method again, as sure as I'm standing here. Now, I know it was an accident when Tag ran that railway line, but the result's exactly the same: he'll know now that running the line will get hounds off his tail, because it's happened—he's proved it. So he'll do it *again* and *again*, and we're going to lose more hounds and *still* more hounds...don't you see, I've simply got to kill him! I've got to!"

Kendrick was silent for a long time, staring moodily into the fire. Then he sighed deeply and rubbed his forehead.

"I'm sorry, Asher," he said at last, "I owe you an apology. All I can say is, if I did a bit more listening and a bit less talking, I'd probably know a lot more than I do."

Kendrick looked very old, all of a sudden.

"And there's more yet—" Asher went on, more quietly now, "There's Merlin, as well..."

"Merlin? What's wrong with him?"

Asher slumped back into his chair, frowning as he groped for words:

"Poor old dog—he just doesn't know which side he's supposed to be on when we're hunting his old mate. It wasn't so bad when he could lead the pack, but he's getting old, now, and slowing down... and there's me, as well."

Kendrick looked up, startled.

"You?"

"Aye, the whole thing's getting me down. I'm not doing my job as well as I ought—and I'm not always fair to young Stephen, either..."

Asher's voice trailed off and both men were silent for a while. It was Kendrick who broke the spell.

"Well," he said briskly, "that's that, then. We'd better organize a drive and shoot him—"

Asher's reaction was immediate and passionate:

"No, sir, not that way—you can't."

"What? Why not, man?"

"I don't know, but it'd be a terrible wrong. Something to do with... honor, or something. I've got to hunt him and kill him above ground, fair and square."

"But, look here—"

"No, sir! It's got to be that way, or else it's no good."

Chapter Seventeen

WHEN STEPHEN REALIZED that Asher would be laid up for a while, he felt a fierce surge of joy at the prospect of carrying the horn. In all the nine years he had whipped-in to Asher, the little man had never missed a single day's hunting. Stephen had had his quota of days off for sickness, and so had Frank Sammells, but not the huntsman... Asher seemed to be made of a different material from other people, and was only ever slowed down by illness— never stopped. But this time...

Although Asher should have been in bed, he preferred to be in the kennels. On the Tuesday—the day before Stephen was to take over and hunt hounds—Asher could sense the young man's fierce, secret joy. He had long been aware of Stephen's impatience to take over, but had never fully realized the intensity of the young man's ambition—and now the realization upset him. He had carefully rehearsed a little talk to be delivered in the valeting-room that evening: a few selected Do's and Don'ts, followed by his sincere good wishes for a successful day—but in the end he couldn't go through with it. Feeling awkward, and somewhat ashamed of himself, he slipped out of the kennels and back into the house, without even bidding the young man good night. Stephen noticed this omission and—

naturally—misinterpreted it. His determination to make a success of his début hardened still more.

The following morning Asher helped in the kennels as usual, but after breakfast he stayed in the house and was not present when Stephen left with the hounds. He didn't want to appear churlish, but he couldn't fully trust himself not to come out with something, so, in the end, he decided to keep out of temptation's way.

It was not until after lunch, when he heard Merlin's mournful howling, that he realized that Stephen had left the old hound at home. Something snapped within him—some resistance that had caused him to half-blame the old hound for the death of the other seven. He understood suddenly how Merlin must have been feeling, and was overcome with remorse. He went straight to the lodging-room and walked in—Merlin looked at him as he entered and then turned his head away. Asher went over and sat beside him in the straw. For ten minutes he talked to the old hound in his soft voice, and all the while Merlin kept his head turned away from him. At last he seemed to get through: Merlin turned his head slowly until he was looking full at Asher from his deep golden-brown eyes. He held the look for more than a minute, then put his head gently in Asher's lap and mourned quietly, trembling all over. Asher stroked the old hound's fine head and fondled the long ears and whispered to him until it was all out, and he had stopped trembling. When at last he had to leave, to go and prepare the oatmeal, Merlin was his old self again.

Stephen was lucky. Scenting conditions were good; the hounds worked well for him; they had a good day's hunting and killed in the afternoon. Everyone remarked how nice he looked and were

impressed by his voice. Stephen made a good job of
it, and his frank, pleasant manner charmed people
who had grown used to Asher's taciturnity and utter
absorption in his hounds. During the day, a number
of people went up to the young man and congratu-
lated him on his ability; one or two even intimated
that he was a welcome change and hoped they'd see
him carrying the horn again. Stephen was already in
a condition of mild euphoria after the day's
excitement, and this touch of adulation completed
the process. Frank Sammells—who had stood in as
whipper-in—was the first to come up against it,
right at the end of the day. Stephen was talking
animatedly to a lady wearing side-saddle habit—a
member of the Hunt Committee—and Frank was
just easing his aching seat-bones, long unaccus-
tomed to the saddle. The hounds were gathered
loosely round them, weary and contented; most of
them were sitting on their haunches, but one or two
were wandering aimlessly—suddenly Frank jumped
as Stephen's voice rapped out:

"Sammells!"

The kennelman turned, startled, to see Stephen
glaring at him, his face flushed with anger. He was
so surprised that he failed to reply and simply stared
back, open-mouthed—this made Stephen angrier
still:

"Watch the hounds, man! They're wandering all
over the countryside."

Frank turned automatically to obey and Stephen
resumed his conversation with the lady—who now
looked faintly embarrassed, although Stephen
failed to notice this. *Well, well, well* . . . Frank was
thinking amiably, as he herded the hounds together,
getting the bit stick out, eh? He smiled grimly—*I
hope I'm there the first time you try using it on our
Asher* . . .

* * *

As soon as hounds had been fed, Stephen went in to report to Asher. He was still a few inches above the ground and was not as tactful as he might have been, but Asher put this down to an understandable excitement, and resolved not to take offence. Towards the end of the session, however, this resolve was stretching alarmingly thin. So elated was the young man that he was almost beginning to believe he could do a better job of hunting hounds. This feeling was coming through fairly strongly to Asher, who had to bite back the dressing-down he felt the young man badly needed. Just before leaving, Stephen made one last comment that almost snapped Asher's restraint:

"By the way," he said airily, "d'you remember we had a discussion once about forward casts at the gallop, and you warned me against them? Well, I tried three or four today and hit him off every time—in fact, they wouldn't have killed if it hadn't been for the last one."

There was a strained silence, then:

"I'm glad they worked for you," Asher replied carefully, clenching and unclenching his fists behind his back.

The following morning, Asher obtained an interview with Kendrick and asked if he could resume his duties as huntsman, straight away.

"Don't be ridiculous, Ash," Kendrick snorted. "It's out of the question. The doc said a couple of weeks at least—remember?"

Asher fought to control his rising anger.

"I'm feeling one hundred per cent and I'd like to carry on, sir," he said.

Kendrick swung round and peered at him over his glasses:

"You've had my answer," he said quietly.

"But I'm all right," Asher persisted, "and I don't want—"

"What's happened to you!" Kendrick exploded. "I've never known you like this before—what's the matter with you?"

"Nothing's the matter," Asher replied, his voice shaking with suppressed anger. "I just want to get back to my job."

"And I've told you—" Kendrick roared—"you're not going to until you're fit—is that clear?"

Asher's face was deathly pale and his whole frame was trembling. The two men stood face to face for several seconds, staring at each other—and it was Kendrick who turned away, in the end. He stumped over to his desk and flopped down into his swivel-chair with an exasperated sigh.

"I don't know—" he was muttering. "Never known you like this, Ash—what's eating you, anyway—" Then he broke off and looked up, sharply. "Is it young Stephen?" he asked, without warning. Asher must have given himself away, for Kendrick banged his fist triumphantly on the desktop.

"So that's it!" he exclaimed.

Asher looked away and was silent; when Kendrick spoke again, his voice was quiet and sympathetic.

"The young tyke—" he said, "giving you a rough time, is he?"

"It's not that, really—" Asher hesitated, and Kendrick went on equably:

"All right, Ash, we'll say it's not that—but look here, old lad, I can't let you jump straight back into the saddle, can I? I mean, that was quite a purler you took. Now look—you let Stephen carry on on Saturday, then you come and see me on Monday morning: if I think you're fit, you can take over again on Tuesday. Fair enough?"

And with that Asher had to be content.

Stephen's second experience of hunting hounds, that Saturday, was as different from his first as it could have been. The day dawned dry and clear, but a blustery west wind was getting up and growing stronger all the time. From the moment they left the kennels, the hounds seemed to be possessed of a capricious corporate spirit. At first Frank Sammells charged assiduously here and there, rounding up the miscreants, but after half an hour both he and his horse were blown, and when—for the fiftieth time—Stephen ordered him to put the hounds on to him again, Frank stuck his heels in:

"Look here, Steve," he grumbled, "you'll have us knackered afore we get to the meet, even—now you just settle down a bit and let's get along as best we can."

The first covert was blank, and so was the second; when they found a fox in the third, he ran them out of scent inside six or seven fields; while hunting that one, three couple of hounds went off after a hare that jumped up under their noses, and Frank had no chance of getting to their heads; when another fox went away from the next covert, Stephen blew his horn for five minutes and only three and a half couple came out to see what was happening. By the end of the afternoon, the young man was in a towering rage, and when one of the ebullient hounds made a dive at a ginger cat that shot out of a hedgerow and scorched up a nearby tree, he finally lost control.

"Tester!" he yelled, as he aimed his whip-lash at the offender's rump. "What d'you think you're doing!"

The lash curled round Tester's ribs, and the young hound promptly bolted, screaming blue murder as he went. Stephen turned, his face scarlet with anger:

"Sammells—get after that hound!" he shouted. The old kennelman grinned amiably and cantered off after the truant, while Stephen trotted on in a surly silence. Fifty yards behind, Kendrick was fighting a losing battle with an angelic smile that kept spreading across his face. He looked round guiltily as one of the "regulars" jogged up alongside him.

"Ah—morning, Kelting," he said, with more than his usual joviality. "Bit windy, eh?"

"Certainly is, Master. I say—Young Durno's having a bit of a time of it, isn't he?"

The angelic smile creased Kendrick's face yet again:

"Yes he is, isn't he?" he agreed, happily.

"Never seen Asher having this sort of trouble."

Kendrick's smile widened even more:

"No," he chuckled, "neither have I . . ."

That evening, after the hounds had been fed and put away, Asher waited patiently for Stephen to come in and make his report . . . at half-past seven he decided that the young man would not be showing up, and at twenty to eight, Stephen arrived.

"I'm sorry, sir," he said, without preamble, "I made an awful hash of it."

This uncompromising statement went straight through Asher's defenses—he had armed himself with a shield of reserve and a sword of righteousness after Kendrick had told him—gleefully—of the day's happenings; but Stephen's honesty broke through his reserve and dispelled his righteousness, at a single blow.

"Well..." Asher extemporized, hurriedly, "you couldn't have chosen a much worse day to take hounds out, after all."

"I suppose not," Stephen muttered, but he was still very gloomy. The two men were silent for a few moments, as each waited for the other to speak—then Stephen pulled himself together with a visible effort.

"Well," he said, turning towards the door, "I'd better be off."

Asher made up his mind.

"Stephen," he said.

The young man turned and looked at him: his face, usually so alive, was empty of expression. Asher went on, speaking softly, yet with an intensity that made his eyes seem to burn like coals in their deep sockets:

"If I didn't think much of a chap—I mean, if I knew he'd never make a good huntsman, you know what I'd do?"

Stephen shook his head, mystified.

"I'd jolly him along," Asher said. "If he did something wrong, I'd say 'Not to worry, old lad—just try a bit harder,' or something like that—see?"

Stephen nodded, listening carefully.

"But," Asher went on, "if I had a young chap that I thought a lot of ... and if I felt, deep down, that he might possibly make a great huntsman one day—and I mean a *great* huntsman—d'you know what I'd do then?"

Stephen did not move—he was following Asher's words with every last atom of concentration, and as he listened, his face was coming slowly to life...

"I'll tell you what I'd do then, Stephen Durno—I'd bully him, and push him around, and make him feel small, and pick him up on every last thing—and I'd go on doing that until he began to really hate my guts—and you know what that would do? It'd make him fight back—make him work his heart out to beat me—make him learn his job so damn well that I couldn't find fault, and then start learning *mine*!"

He paused to let this sink in, never taking his burning eyes off the young man's face; after a few moments he went on:

"And last of all, I'd try to get to the bottom of him... I'd want to find out whether he had a breaking point, where he suddenly runs away from what he can't take any longer, or whether he faces it right to the bitter end and then comes back for more... that's what I'd do, if I really believed in him. Do you understand Stephen?"

Conflicting emotions were chasing each other across the young man's face—he thought he understood, but could find no words for the moment.

"The day before yesterday," Asher said, "you proved two things to me: one was that my hounds can hunt themselves and the other was that you cut a dashing figure with a hunting-horn in your hand... but today—" he broke off and repeated:

"*Today*—you showed me what you're finally made of. When you walked in through that door, just now, and said what you did, that's all I needed to know. You're going to be all right, lad."

That night, over supper, Asher said:

"I had a talk with Stephen this evening, Cathie."

She jumped, as though startled, and looked at him with frightened, questioning eyes—he noticed her reaction and smiled.

"It's all right, love," he said. "It was a friendly chat—not what you were thinking."

"Oh, Asher..." she said, letting her breath out in a rush, "you gave me such a turn. I thought you'd—"

"I know," he said, and touched her arm gently, asking her forgiveness. "I shouldn't have done that—I'm sorry, Cathie."

"It's all right," she laughed, breathlessly. "You know me and my imagination—"

"I ought to, by now," he replied, as he got on with his meal.

Cathie was withdrawn and thoughtful for a while, and they ate slowly in their own separate silences—then she laid her knife and fork down and leaned towards Asher:

"Does that mean—" she began.

"Does what mean?" he interrupted, absently.

"What you said about talking to Stephen—does that mean...well, that everything's all right between you?"

Asher raised his eyebrows at her.

"Why, was anything wrong?" he asked.

"Oh, Asher—you know what I mean."

"Stephen and I get on very well together, nearly all the time," Asher said, smiling on the side she couldn't see.

"Does that mean—" Cathie went on, pursuing her point to the end, "that you don't mind about him and Jenny—"

"What about him and Jenny?" Asher snapped, turning on her like a striking snake. Cathie was flustered by his sudden anger: she blushed and groped for words.

"Well, you said...I was wondering about Jenny, and—"

"It's all in your imagination, Cathie," he said, angrily, "the whole thing is all in your head!"

He stood up, pushing his chair back sharply so that it almost fell.

"I'm going out," he said.

*　　*　　*

Ever since the night of the accident, when Asher told Tod that he would have to kill Tag, the huntsman had felt a deep-lying sadness that lay underneath everything he said, or did, or thought. The old man had not come back after that evening, and Asher knew that he would be feeling the same sadness—only more strongly, perhaps, for he was a lonely, proud old man and his friendship with Asher was his last remaining point of contact with humanity...for, apart from this one relationship, all the weight of the old man's lifetime of unused, unwanted love had at last found an outlet, and was now being lavished on the survival of a wild fox...

Asher found him where he knew he would: in the smoke-hazy parlor of the Carrington Arms, in Cawsdon. When Tod looked up and saw Asher standing in front of him, he started violently, then scowled and looked away.

"Come on, Tod," Asher said, without preamble, "I want to talk to you."

The old man said nothing, but drained his mug and left with Asher.

The night was mild and a soft blanket of cloud hid the moon. A few late bats were flickering drowsily across the road, but otherwise there was only the sound of their footsteps. They walked in silence for a while as Asher tried to gather his thoughts. He wanted desperately to make contact with the silent old man, just as Jenny had needed to get through to him a little while ago—only Jenny had a way of finding the right words when they were needed, while Asher—who could cast spells over animals with the magic of his voice—lacked the gift with his own species, and fumbled like the rest of them. At last, in desperation, he blurted out:

"Tod, I've got to kill that fox—isn't it obvious?"

He expected the old man to shout, or argue, or

plead—anything but the one word he actually said:
"Why?"

"Because he'll kill more of my hounds, and then more, if I don't—you know that, Tod! You *know* a fox'll always play the same trick over if it works the first time."

He waited anxiously for the old man to say *It's all right, I understand* . . . to say *Go ahead, I know you've got to do it* . . . to say *I know you don't want to do it, and I forgive you* . . . to say anything—yet again—except what he finally said:

"Yer can't do it, Asher."

The huntsman stopped in his tracks, unable for the moment to absorb what he had heard—for long moments he fumbled, then he exploded:

"But, Tod—for heaven's sake! I've explained—you know I've got to do it . . ."

But the old man was shaking his great, shaggy head.

"It don't change a thing," he said, "yer can't do it."

Asher was still groping helplessly for words when Tod's whole manner changed, startlingly—he grabbed the huntsman's arms and held him in a fierce grip as a flood of words started to pour out of him:

"Listen, Asher—I know he'll do it again, so I've worked it out so's you don't have to kill him: no—" he hung on savagely as Asher tried to turn away from him. "Listen," he gabbled on, "I've been feeding 'em for a couple of years now—I know where he is an' I know where he goes, every minute of every day. Listen, it's easy—" Again Asher tried to break free, but Tod was like a man possessed. "Every night before yer go hunting, I can put 'im to ground, see? If I get too matey with 'im, he always slips down the nearest earth. I can stop 'em in, then, and leave some grub with 'im until yer come home from hunting, then untop it and let 'im out—he'll soon get used to it, see? Anyway, he don't enjoy being hunted like he used to . . . It'll work, Asher, I know it will—an' yer won't have to kill 'im . . ."

He tailed off at last, and his hands fell from Asher's arms. Only his eyes waited, beseechingly, for Tag's reprieve . . . Asher felt pity and a sadness beyond measure as he answered gently:

"It's no good, Tod—it won't do. I can't risk it ever happening again."

He waited, but the old man was silent—and even as Asher watched, he seemed to shrink in upon himself a little, staring down at the ground. At last he spoke, still with his eyes averted, in a voice so low that Asher had to strain his ears to hear it:

"Don't do it, Asher, please . . . I'm an old man and that fox and you are the only two things I've got that I care anything for. Don't take 'em both away from me. Please . . ."

"Tod, I don't—"

"Please, Asher—" the old man looked up into his eyes, imploring him: "please give him a chance."

Asher could take no more: he turned away.

"It's no use," he said for the last time, "I've got to do it, Tod."

He walked away then, unable to bear the old man's agony, leaving him standing in the middle of the road.

At ten o'clock on Monday morning, Asher appeared before Kendrick, as arranged; he asked for, and—after a certain amount of hesitation—finally got what he wanted: permission to take the horn again for the following day's hunting.

That afternoon he handed the kennels over to Frank and Stephen and went off in the car, without

saying where he was going. He returned soon after
eight o'clock, muddy and very tired—for he was still
weak from the effects of his recent fall. He ate his
supper with a preoccupied air and went out
immediately afterwards—again, without a word of
explanation.

Cathie was worried about him: he looked so
weary, and yet so taut—as though he were
dangerously near breaking-point. She went to bed
just before midnight and somewhere around 3 a.m.
Asher came back. When he finally sank into bed
beside her he fell asleep immediately, and then
began to stir restlessly moaning and breathing
noisily. Once she reached across and laid her hand
on his forehead: it was damp with sweat and hot to
the touch.

In the morning it was obvious Asher was
sickening for something, but he brushed aside her
one weak attempt to persuade him not to go out
hunting.

"I'll be all right, love," he said absent-mindedly,
"it's just a cold or something."

Cathie thought not, but could say no more.

Chapter Eighteen

THE MEET THAT day was the lawn Meet at the big house itself, at which Kendrick himself entertained the Hunt. The mild spell of weather had broken up and it was bitterly cold; an easterly wind was blowing occasional flurries of sleet and the forecast had promised snow. In spite of this it could still be a good day's hunting because the prevailing conditions appeared to be favorable to scent.

Asher positioned the hounds against one of the six-foot yew hedges that bordered the flanks of the lawn in front of the big house. He looked down at the hounds as they moved around him and singled out Merlin: the old hound had been almost hysterical with joy when he had realized that he would be going out with the pack again. As Asher caught his eye, Merlin returned the look, waving his tail. Looking over the rest of the pack, Asher felt yet again the sense of loss that had haunted him since the death of his best young hounds. Their names went through his mind as though they were being read out in a memorial service: Dasher, Harlequin, Marksman, Prophet and Priestess, Whimsy and Talisman... he saw them with his mind's eye, as clearly as though they were still there: radiant and eager, bursting with health and life... and then the vision faded and he saw them again, broken, twisted and bloody...He shivered violently and looked down to see that Kendrick was there and had apparently said something to him—

"I'm sorry," he said, "I didn't catch that."

"I was asking you how you felt."

"Very well, thank you, sir."

"You're quite sure you're fit to do a day's hunting? I mean, if you aren't a hundred per cent, you'd better say so, right away."

"No, I'll be all right, sir—but thank you anyway."

Kendrick smiled up at him with his quick, lopsided smile and touched Asher's knee with a white-gloved hand.

"Good luck, then, my old Ash," he said, and walked off towards his horse, which was being held by the head groom.

When Kendrick was on his horse and settled, Asher touched his horn and walked forward, with Stephen behind him. As soon as he pushed his horse on into a jog-trot, Asher felt sudden pains in his chest and back—grimly he settled down to ride as though they weren't there, hoping desperately that they would not slow him down.

The first draw of the day was a medium-sized spinney, not far from the house. They drew it blank and Asher called his hounds out and turned his horse towards the great dark mass of Kennel Wood.

He knew that Tag was there—he'd known since three days' before, when he had seen the old fox's distinctive pad-marks crossing one of the rides. As the wood loomed closer he felt a knot of tension deep within himself: a kind of helplessness, as though he were being swept along by events which he could not control.

He saw a figure standing beside the main ride that led into the wood, and knew that it was Tod. The feeling of fate became even stronger as he saw the old man's eyes boring into him, sad and accusing at the same time. He wanted to say something to him, to reassure him—to explain that he was no longer in control of events and that what must happen must happen—but the moment had passed, and the lonely figure of the old man was dropping back behind them as they entered the covert.

"Leu in then," he said quietly. "Leu in."

The hounds flew into the undergrowth and were out of sight within seconds. He heard the receding sounds of their progress as they began to draw the great wood.

In the echoing stillness with the great silent trees all round him, Asher sensed his own final surrender to whatever had taken him over. He was filled suddenly with a confusion of emotions and thoughts, like colors whirling. He felt wide open, suddenly—as open as the woods around him, and as filled with life and death... he experienced fleeting sensations of an extraordinary sweetness that brought tears to his eyes, and he wondered if perhaps he was going mad. But no, there was this *rightness* about everything... whatever he did on this fateful day would be the right thing to do—he had only to play his part and the pattern—unfinished for so long—would be complete and whole. With all his heart, he cheered his hounds:

"Yoi try-hy! Yoi try-hy-y-y-y!"

He felt light and insubstantial, yet strong and certain. The voice with which he cheered his hounds rang out and echoed through the woods in spreading ripples of pure sound:

"Yoi try wind 'im the-e-e-e-re!"

He *knew* suddenly... he had no hatred for the Belstone Fox, yet he had to find him and hunt him. The answer would be at the end of the hunt... the answer, which could be either life or death.

"Yoi try-hy-y-y-y!"

A quarter of a mile away, Kendrick listened again to the distant sound of Asher's voice: he caught his breath at the sheer, thrilling beauty of it. He looked round and saw that others had noticed it, too, and were listening, entranced...

"Yoi try wind 'im the-e-e-e-re!"

Far away, in the depths of the wood, a whimper...a pause, and then another, stronger than before—a strange excitement was born somewhere in Asher's guts and again he *knew*...

"Hark 'ark 'ark 'ark to Merlin! Yoi at 'im Merlin!"

He doubled the horn, blowing the quick repeated notes that would tell the hounds that something was afoot, and urged his horse on towards the center of the wood. Merlin spoke again, with more conviction this time, and the next moment there was a burst of music as a few more hounds joined the old dog-hound and spoke to the line. Asher doubled the horn again and pushed on into a canter: he felt pains tearing across his chest and shoulders but they seemed unimportant, as if they were hurting somebody else. The cry of the hounds rang out louder and more certain. He heard Stephen's voice, from up ahead, hollering:

"Over-over-over-over-over-r-r!"

He galloped forward along the ride and pulled up beside the whipper-in.

"Is it him?" he asked.

"Yes, sir, I think so."

Asher galloped on past him doubling his horn again and yet again as more and more hounds flew to support the few who owned the line, swelling the music until at last the full chorus of the pack crashed out, echoing from end to end of the great wood.

* * *

Tag was running—not afraid but strong in the intensity of his determination to escape. He slipped eel-like through the tangled undergrowth, going no faster than he need. He went swiftly to the nearest earth and ran on without a pause when he saw that it had been stopped.

Tod knew that Asher had stopped every earth within conceivable reach of Kennel Wood—knew that the huntsman, weak as he was, had done it single-handed the previous night. It would have been easy for the old man to unstop the earths behind him, but for one thing: it was vital that Tag should *not* go to ground for if he did Asher would be able to put the terriers down and dig him out. Tod knew that the old fox must take his chance above the ground.

Tag ran past the last earth with hardly a glance, as though he knew that it would be stopped like all the others. With the cry of the hounds drawing closer every minute, he headed for the far side of the wood.

After Asher had passed him, looking haggard and intense, Tod hurried round to where the ground rose gently, lifting the wood like Sargasso weed in a gentle swell. Here he stood waiting, following the progress of the invisible hounds as their music echoed round the covert. He heard the rise in pitch and excitement as they drew closer to the hunted fox, and knew that Tag would be forced to break cover before long.

He caught his breath as a speck of red burst from the wall of undergrowth two hundred yards away and streaked across the grass on a course that would pass close to where he stood. He waited tensely for a holler, but there was no sound apart from the hounds, still hunting the line inside the covert. As

Tag approached he saw that the old fox was going with a shortened stride and his heart yearned suddenly towards him, knowing the pain of limbs that will not flex and swing as once they did—knowing the agony of lungs that burn and a heart that labors to pump blood that used to sing unbidden through the veins. Tag saw him suddenly: his ears pricked, his stride faltered and he looked straight at the old man...For one unbelieving second Tod thought that he was going to run to him—dreamed a wild dream of snatching up the beloved red body and running for sanctuary with Tag hidden deep in the breast of his overcoat...but the next instant the old fox ran on, his ears flattened, his brush streaming out behind like the tail of a comet, and at the same moment the leading hounds erupted from the wood on his line. The old man watched as Tag leaped the ditch and scrambled through the fence, on the far side of the field. He caught another glimpse of him as he ran up a furrow in the adjoining plough, and then no more. Something broke suddenly, within him, and with tears blurring his vision, he shouted uselessly after the running fox:

"I wish I could run for yer!"

Asher heard the abrupt change in the timbre of the music as the pack ran out into the open—the echoes died as suddenly as though they had been cut off. He sent his horse on and swung sharply to the right, down one of the intersecting rides. He heard the pack settling down and hunting steadily away from the wood, and at the same time Stephen's voice in the distance:

"Forrard awa-a-a-a-a-ay!"

The five-bar gate loomed up in front of him, showing black against the light outside the wood.

He checked his horse, out of habit, then drove it forward fiercely, unable to curb his impatience. The big bay took off early and cleared the top bar with inches to spare—even as it landed Asher was pulling the horn from his coat. He blew the "Gone away" as he galloped on across the pasture towards where the tail-hounds were just leaping or scrambling over the hedge, behind the body of the pack.

The sensation of unreality had left him for the moment, as every atom of his consciousness was caught up in the violence of his forward movement. The total capacities of his mind and body were channelled into the one obsessive endeavor: to follow his hounds as they hunted the Belstone Fox for the last time.

So absolute was his absorption that he passed within yards of Tod without even seeing him.

Kendrick heard Asher blow the "Gone away" and moved forward down the ride, with a hundred and twenty riders behind him. As they surged out into the open, some of the more enthusiastic of them galloped forward on either side but Kendrick would have none of it:

"Hold hard!" he bellowed. "I'll tell you when!"

I'll hold 'em as long as I can he thought *but once they get going today it'll be devil take the hindmost . . .*

He saw Asher jump out of the plough, a field ahead, and suddenly kicked his horse on, catching most of the field by surprise. For fifty yards he was on his own, but as he felt his old gray gather itself for the fence in front, he heard the thunder of hooves close behind him and thought *Here we go!*

Asher's brain was crystal clear. His body felt as though it had no substance; his hearing and his eyesight, too, were affected by the fever, but his disembodied mind was sharp and matter-of-fact as he watched the flying pack ahead of him and thought his way into the mind of their invisible quarry. He knew that Tag was running across the wind because he was trying to get to the earth in the Roborough Dyke; he also know that this earth, like all the others, was stopped. He guessed that in the ensuing indecision Tag would turn and run down wind pressured by the nearness of the pack into making a dangerous move—for that way lay a stretch of open country with neither covert nor earth to offer him shelter.

Tag saw that the earth was stopped as soon as he reached the opposite bank. He stood for a second or two looking irresolutely from side to side, then the wind carried the fragment of the hounds' cry to his ears and he hesitated no longer. He scrambled to the bottom of the bank in a miniature landslide of loose soil and, turning right-handed, splashed off along the bed of the dyke, running *into* the wind...

Less than a minute later the hounds arrived at the same place. The leaders jumped to the far bank and their cry faltered and ceased as they lost the line. They began to fan out, noses down, as the rest of the pack leaped the dyke and joined them, Merlin among them.

As soon as Asher saw that they had checked, and while still half a field away, he took out his horn and blew a series of quick notes: at the same time he swung his horse diagonally down wind, so that the hounds started to move towards him, they were beginning a down-wind cast, along the dyke bank. So certain was Asher that he had correctly divined the fox's movements that for once he paid no attention to Merlin, who was feathering along the side of the dyke in the opposite direction. Seeing the rest of the pack casting away from him, towards Asher, the old hound turned reluctantly and went with them.

Kendrick pulled his horse up and faced it into the wind to help it catch its breath. He needed a breather himself, and mopped his brow with a large red and white polka-dotted kerchief, hot in spite of the cold day. More riders were struggling up every moment—looking around he guessed that eighty or so were still on terms after the first burst. He looked up then, and noticed the heavy laden sky that seemed to be weighing down on the colorless land. *Snow,* he thought, *Oh no.*

Asher was at a loss—he had swung them in two semi-circles with a lengthening radius and still there was no sign of the line. He looked across at Merlin, then, noticed suddenly how the old hound kept looking back towards the blocked earth... *Up wind* he thought—*Fool! Why didn't I leave it to him, like I always do?* he blew an urgent summons and cantered back along the dyke, with Merlin ahead of him. He slowed to a walk and encouraged them along the banks, talking to them softly to keep their spirits up without distracting them. He saw Merlin's tail wave—then again, and a faint whimper: that was all he needed.

"Hark 'ark to Merlin!" he cheered. "Yoi at 'im, old dog!"

And suddenly they were surging forward again, hunting along the dyke bottom—not as quickly as before, but with authority.

Tag clambered up the steep bank and shook himself, then went on at an easy lope across a grass field. He had gained at least four minutes through Asher's wrong cast, and he went as easily as he could to give his tired body a chance to recuperate.

A group of bullocks, who had been grazing in the field, saw him and cantered over to investigate. He paid no attention to them, so they started to chase after him, frisking and kicking with their tails held high in the air. He grinned malevolently over his shoulder at them but they kept their distance and skittered to a halt, wide-eyed, as he slipped through the hedge, out of their sight.

Tag found himself on the verge beside a road. He turned left and began to run along the road-side at a steady lope, his nose wrinkling in disgust at the lingering diesel and oil smells that permeated everything. A quarter of a mile farther on he saw a lorry coming towards him in the distance—he melted off the road, under the bottom strand of a barbed-wire fence, and into a small spinney.

Asher's chest was a tangled mass of pain; his breath rasped in his throat and there was a singing in his ears but his brain still hovered a little way above all this—ice-calm and detached. In an impersonal way he noticed also that he was shivering and that his grip on the saddle appeared to be loose, but it all seemed rather unimportant. Once Stephen saw him sway in the saddle and thought that he was going to fall, but he recovered and went on as though nothing were wrong.

Merlin kept the lead along the Roborough Dyke, and swung left at the exact spot where Tag had left the shelter of the dyke for open country again, but as soon as they were hunting across the grass, the younger and fitter hounds were passing him one by one. Asher had noticed the sudden movement of the bullocks in the distance so when the leading hounds checked at the edge of the field in which they stood, he was certain of Tag's line: he galloped forward

with a peremptory summons on the horn and
hounds lifted their heads and flew after him with
absolute trust. He swung them along the hedge and
felt a sharp sense of relief when they spoke again. He
popped over the hedge on to the grass verge jumping
from a trot to avoid the risk of slipping on the
tarmac. Hounds faulted again immediately, but not
before he had seen one or two trusted heads
swinging to the left. He touched his horn and set off
along the road at a trot, looking for Worry, who was
his specialist at hunting a line along a road. Sure
enough she wormed her way to the front and took
the lead, her wrinkled face screwed up in the effort
of concentration, throwing tongue in little yelps and
whimpers while the rest of the pack followed in
almost total silence. Asher cursed to himself when a
car passed, forcing him to shepherd the hounds on
to the verge, but old Worry picked it up again and
they went on. A hundred yards farther on, Asher
saw her falter and turn; he reigned in and looked for
Merlin, and even as he found him, the old dog-
hound gave tongue and plunged into the spinney
that stood by the roadside. Within seconds he was
out on the far side and going at top speed across the
grass with the rest of the pack on his heels. Asher's
horse jumped awkwardly off the road and pecked
on landing—the huntsman nearly fell, but just
managed to save himself. In spite of this his heart
was light as he settled himself back in the saddle, for
the hounds were going with a beautiful cry again
and he knew that his fox could not be far ahead.

Tag heard the renewed cry behind him and tried
to accelerate, but his limbs refused to respond. The
effects of the long run of the previous week were
beginning to tell on him: that and old age,
combined. Ahead of him lay a stretch of open

country; there was no shelter nearer than Selby Gorse, which was two miles away on the far side of the Vale. For the second time, Tag set his mask for the Vale—but this time he was already a sinking fox.

Asher felt the first flurry of sleet against his face and offered up a silent prayer that the weather would not close down on them. He could still see the hounds, half a field ahead, but only as a blur of moving whites and browns. Their cry came back to him in fragments, torn off by the fitful wind.

A fence loomed up ahead: a stiff stake-and-bind with a wide ditch in front. He waited for his horse to lengthen its stride, but it was laboring heavily and failed to do so—almost too late he kicked it on: it stretched out for one long stride and then took off, feet too soon. Asher knew that they would hit the fence: heard the crackle and felt the lurch and tumble of a fall, yet the horse saved itself somehow—found an extra leg from somewhere and slid for yards on its knees before struggling to its feet with a grunt and carrying on. Asher was shaken.

"Come on, lad," he whispered, "you've got to hold up now!"

He peered ahead towards the pack, and a sudden gap between showers gave him a clear glimpse: they were running well, and so fast that Merlin was already more than half-way towards the back.

If it keeps going this way, we've got him, he thought—with no exultation, merely a calm acceptance; but even as he thought it, the leading hounds swung a few degrees to the right, faltered and then surged forward again. Looking across in that direction, Asher saw a dark patch against the hillside and knew Tag had gone there. He urged his tiring horse on to a faster pace, with a feeling of certainty taking root in his mind as he looked at the approaching covert.

It was only a patch of rough gorse and bracken, of not more than three or four acres in extent. Tag toiled wearily up the slope and plunged into its cover. He found a trail that wound through the dense gorse and trotted along it, barely able to keep going. He must have been somewhere near the middle of the covert when he stumbled across a sleeping fox. The stranger leaped to his feet with a snarl of warning, but Tag was not one for trouble— far from it, in fact: he picked his way round at a careful distance and went on down the trail, his brush dragging the ground. The stranger watched him go, then turned suddenly and stood at gaze, his ears pricked, his nostrils working. He heard it again: the mournful sound of a pack of foxhounds in full cry, and heading his way.

Asher was urging his horse up the hill as the hounds reached the gorse and disappeared into it as though swallowed up. He turned to see where Stephen was, wanting him to go on round the covert to watch from the far side, but the whipper-in was still two fields away, nursing his mount along at a steady trot. Asher reached the edge of the gorse and let his horse stagger to a halt, its lungs working like bellows, its head almost touching the ground, its nostrils red-lined and distended. He was listening intently to the hounds' music—heard it falter, die for a moment, then crash out suddenly with a glorious new strength.

He cursed, and kicked his horse forward into a shambling trot. The cry of the pack rang out as the hounds ran through the covert and Asher pushed his unwilling mount along the bottom side of it. Just as he arrived at the far side, hounds burst out of the top corner and streamed away up the hill, throwing tongue joyously.

He shouted in his frustration and anger. He saw

Stephen appear round the top side and set off after the pack.

"No, no," he cried, "can't you see?"

The next moment, a solitary hound pushed out of the covert only yards away and began to move slowly down the hill, away from the line taken by the rest of the pack: it was Merlin. He was stiff and blown and aching in every joint, but he was the only hound in the pack to ignore the fresh, strong scent, and stick to the line of the Belstone Fox.

Asher started to move down the hill behind the old dog-hound, who was quietly working out the difficult line for himself. With the ending of the violent movement, Asher realized suddenly how weak he was: his vision was blurred and his chest seemed to be on fire—yet still he had the impression of a preternatural clarity of mind. The sleet was whipping unnoticed against his cheek and he was still shivering.

He heard the thud of hooves behind him and turned, surprised, to see that it was the Master.

"What's wrong?" Kendrick asked. "Why aren't you with your hounds?"

Asher had to concentrate hard to understand the question: he pointed up the hill to where the tail-enders were just disappearing over the skyline, with Stephen in close attendance.

"Fresh fox," he explained. "They've changed."

Kendrick frowned, impatiently.

He said, "It can't be helped—come on, then, man, get after your pack!"

But Asher seemed not to hear, and was staring intently after Merlin. Kendrick's patience snapped:

"Asher, get after your pack!"

The huntsman was hurt and bewildered—he wanted to make Kendrick understand that he was hunting the Belstone Fox, not some immature upstart who knew no better—but words were hard to find. He pointed again at old Merlin.

"There's my pack," he said.

"For goodness sake, man, what's wrong with you?" Kendrick shouted, enraged by Asher's stubborn disobedience.

"Nothing's wrong!" Asher flared back at him.

Suddenly Kendrick was quiet, and deadly serious:

"Asher Smith," he said softly, "if you don't do as you're told, then you're no longer hunting my hounds—is that clear?"

Asher shook his head, as though trying to shake water out of his eyes. He was hurt by Kendrick's failure to understand what was so crystal clear to him—what else could he possibly do except what he was doing?

"I'm staying with my pack, sir," he said, and kicked his horse on in Merlin's wake. Kendrick sat absolutely still for a long time, his face empty of expression.

"So be it," he said at last long after Asher had gone; he turned then and urged his horse back up the hill after the rest of the hounds. A part of him understood what Asher was doing and why, and even respected him for doing it, but the other part of him knew that he had done his duty—that he had been left no choice. As he galloped on in Stephen's wake, his heart felt cold and heavy within him.

The Master's horse was fresher than the hunt-horses, for they had been obliged to follow hounds in a wide sweep across difficult country, while Kendrick had been able to take a short cut, choosing the easier going as he went. As a result, he caught up with Stephen after a little more than a mile. As he approached, the young man turned eagerly—and showed his surprise at seeing the Master rather than the huntsman. As Kendrick came up to him, Stephen started to shout:

"Have you seen—"

But Kendrick cut him off with an upraised hand.

"Hold hard!" he snapped.

The young man slowed down, looking anxiously ahead to where hounds were running—then looked down suddenly to see a hunting-horn which Kendrick was thrusting into his left hand. He stared at it blankly.

"Take hold of it!" Kendrick roared. Stephen came to with a jerk and took it, then looked up as the Master said:

"You're hunting hounds, Stephen."

"But sir—where's Asher?"

"Asher's back there somewhere—you're hunting hounds now."

Stephen pulled up and began to turn his horse back towards where they had come from

"But I must stay with him, sir," he protested, still not fully understanding.

"You'll do as you're told, boy!"

The whipper-in stopped, compelled by the naked command in the Master's voice—then he looked down at the slim golden horn in his hand, the symbol of all that he had ever desired . . .

"Get along then!" Kendrick snapped.

Stephen looked at him again: at the lost-looking eyes in the gray, tired face.

"Yes, sir," he said.

He urged his horse on into a gallop, his eyes automatically scanning the country ahead for the flying pack. As he went, he pushed the horn between the second and third buttons on his coat, where it lodged. He didn't look at it again. He saw the shimmering brown and white specks, at least five fields ahead. *My hounds,* he thought: *Huntsman to the Belstone*...

Never before had he known such an aching, desolate misery as now he felt.

Chapter Nineteen

THE THREE PROTAGONISTS were finally alone: united years before in bonds of friendship, and reunited now in a strange, lonely hunt across a darkening landscape.

Tag could hear that he was being hunted by one hound only, but one hound was enough—the game had ended for him the week before, with the leading hounds only yards behind with death in their voices. In deadly earnest, Tag ran for his life on limbs that felt like lead.

The sleet turned to snow, which was blown in fitful gusts across the twilight country. Asher felt it cool and refreshing against his burning face but found that it was getting harder every minute to keep Merlin in sight. The old dog-hound was hunting steadily, loping on at a weary canter—from time to time Asher heard his voice, sounding faraway and mournful. His horse was nearly done, he knew. Although Merlin's progress was steady, it was still necessary to jump fences to stay with him. So far they had been lucky, and Asher had been able to save the tired animal by opening a few gates, but they were running into a bad piece of country with big overgrown hedges and difficult gates.

Tag had been running aimlessly, with no goal in mind, but suddenly the pattern of the dimly-seen landscape touched a chord of memory: he looked at the gray lump of a hill on the skyline and remembered the badger-setts—the deep labyrinth of tunnels into which a dozen hunted foxes could disappear without trace. Although barely able to keep on his feet, the prospect of sanctuary—however distant—gave him new heart, and his pace quickened slightly.

The snow was beginning to settle, and on the windward side of hedges it was already six or seven inches deep. As Asher peered ahead, straining to see the solitary hound, the snowflakes danced and whirled across his vision, making him dizzy. His horse could not go much farther. It was shambling along with its head low, stumbling and swaying with exhaustion. Asher, too, must have been near his limit, but his detached mind hardly noticed his body's distress—it seemed to hover above, looking down at the lonely horseman with the fever-bright eyes in the gaunt, haggard face. He saw a fence looming up out of the murk: a big ugly blackthorn with a dyke in front, back-fenced with barbed wire. He turned and followed its length, looking for a place to jump, or get through, but there was none. He would have to go back on his tracks and make a detour, but he knew that he dare not, for he would lose all contact with Merlin. After moments of agonized indecision, he made up his mind, threw himself off and crawled through the wire, leaped the ditch and forced his way through the dense hedge, his face and clothes torn in a dozen places by the inch-long thorns. He caught a glimpse of the old hound on the far side of the field and set off after him. Behind him, on the other side of the hedge, the abandoned horse stood, its head almost touched the ground, its ribs pumping as it breathed in great draughts of air, limbs spread apart and trembling.

In the gathering darkness, Merlin hunted on. For

him the game was still a game—for him it had not been touched by tragedy, and as he drew closer and yet closer to his old companion his voice became eager and he forced his tired limbs to quicken.

Asher ran, stumbling and lurching in his exhaustion. His top-boots were never designed for running and hampered him badly, but he struggled on, buoyed up by the sheer intensity of his obsession to follow the hunt to its conclusion, whatever that might be. He was less than a hundred yards behind Merlin now, and although it was almost impossible to see the old hound, he was able to follow his steady, patient baying.

Tag came to where the ground began to rise, at the foot of Grimthorpe Hill. He was hardly trotting now, and was leaving a wandering track in the thin carpet of snow. Filthy and bedraggled, his back was up and his brush dragged along the ground; his mouth was shut, but his lips were drawn back in a perpetual snarl of effort.

Asher's mind began to play tricks on him. It left his body to run mechanically on, falling and picking itself up to go on again, while his mind soared above on shimmering winds of fever, looking down through disembodied eyes that pierced the darkness... suddenly he was looking down at Merlin, watching the old dog-hound hunting steadily on, his limbs going like clock-work. His tail was low and his glorious voice was weakening, but his blood was ancient and good as it drove him on, denying the vitiations of old age. Asher felt a surge of pride at the sight—then his mind seemed to be caught up in a vortex which whirled him back and down and into his struggling body: with a shock he experienced again the confused sensations of pain and fatigue from every part of him. He felt a sudden thirst, like a fire burning—without thinking, he dropped to his knees and scooped up a handful of snow and stuffed it into his mouth, then got up and stumbled forward again.

Tag saw the greater darkness of the spinney against the sky. He was walking now—slowly and deliberately, placing one foot forward, then another, then another...and two hundred yards behind him, Merlin, too, had slowed almost to a walk and his voice was a repeated whimper of excitement.

Asher fell, headlong. As he pushed himself up, he saw Merlin's tracks in the snow, and then—with a sense of disbelief—the wavering line of Tag's footprints as well. It was as though he had not, until that moment, fully believed in the fox's existence, for he had not seen him once during the whole hunt. Here, suddenly, was irrefutable evidence, and Asher felt a sense of wonder as he got to his feet and staggered on.

With infinite slowness Tag half walked, half crawled the last fifty yards up the slope. He felt the wind slacken as he came into the lee of the spinney and made for the outcrop of rock at its center, with the cave beneath it. Almost blind with pain, more dead than alive, he dragged himself through the sparse undergrowth towards the cave, driven on by the instinct to survive and nothing else—for there was nothing else left. He felt the sudden change in the air, sensed the deeper blackness and the rock beneath his feet as he entered the mouth of the cave. He pitched forward and lay for a moment, unable to move, his breath whistling through his teeth, then grimly dragged himself over the last few feet to sanctuary: the endless maze of the Grimthorpe badger setts. His nose came up against something solid where there should have been only air.

The hole was blocked.

*   *   *

Merlin entered the spinney. Tag's scent was strong in his nostrils as it clung momentarily to brambles and dead vegetation before blowing away on the cold wind. Had he not been so close to his quarry he could not have followed the line, for a tired fox leaves hardly any scent.

In the cave, Tag heard the noise of Merlin's approach, and as the hound's silhouette appeared in the entrance, he turned at bay. As the old hound lunged forward with a whimper of recognition, Tag tried to get to his feet to defend himself, but he fell back helplessly—the next moment Merlin was licking him all over his face, whimpering ecstatically. In Tag, the instinct to fight died away and recognition took its place: again he tried to stand, but could not, so he lay where he was and licked Merlin when and where he could. Suddenly both animals stopped and turned: a shape loomed up until it almost shut off the dim light of the evening sky, and Asher stood at the cave-mouth.

He stood, swaying slightly, supporting himself with one hand against the side of the cave while his eyes adjusted to the poor light. Then he saw them— Tag lying on his side, with Merlin standing over him. At first he thought that the fox was dead, but then he saw an ear flicker and knew that he must do it himself. So fine-stretched was he by exhaustion and fever that there was room for only one thought in his mind: *The Belstone Fox must die...* He moved forward towards the two animals, his eyes fixed on the bedraggled ruff round Tag's neck, his hands out in front of him, the fingers crooked and tense. Again Tag tried to move as fear stirred in him, for the shape that loomed towards him had the look of death about it—but again he failed. As Asher's hands moved towards him, Tag snarled silently and his eyes did not waver... suddenly Asher stopped, with his hands a yard from the fox's throat—he stayed like that for a moment, swaying, then pitched forward on to his face, almost on top of the two animals.

The snow had stopped and the sky was clear and bright with stars. A new moon shone with a pale radiance over the winter landscape. The snow that lay against the hedges and powdered the open ground reflected the moonlight and emphasized the blackness of the trees and hedgerows.

Inside the cave, Asher lay where he had fallen. He was breathing rapidly and with difficulty and the whole of his body was shivering spasmodically. The air in the cave was a fraction below freezing-point: with his resistance lowered by a combination of exhaustion and incipient pneumonia, Asher was not far away from death—and every minute, every hour, would see him a little closer.

The two animals lay together, to one side. They had slept fitfully, twitching and moaning in an exhausted coma, but first Tag woke and then Merlin, and for a while they lay close together in a companionable silence. Suddenly the old hound became aware of the inert form of Asher: he got up and went across to him, then sniffed at the huntsman's face and licked the hand that rested on the cold ground in front of him. When there was no response, he whined anxiously and looked around at Tag, as though expecting help. For a while he stood unhappily over the unconscious man, whining almost inaudibly, and then seemed to come to a decision: turning round a couple of times, he lay down with his curled body against Asher's stomach. After watching him for some minutes, Tag stood up and walked stiffly over to join him; the old fox sniffed carefully at Asher's face, then lay down beside Merlin, turning a couple of times in the same way before snuggling down against the huntsman's chest. For a while the two animals licked each other, for mutual comfort, but weariness was creeping up their limbs and along their aching bodies.

As the night deepened and became brittle with stars, sleep overtook them again and they lay, curled close together, within the curve of the huntsman's body.

Long before the Hunt had disappeared into the distance, Tod was hurrying in its wake—although not on exactly the same course: he knew that the earth in Roborough Dyke was stopped and guessed that Tag would eventually be forced to swing down wind, so he set off across the country in the direction of the Vale.

An hour and a half later he was on the road that drops down the hill on the north side of the Vale, before it swings southwest, towards Harberton. Looking out across the patchwork of green and shades of brown, he could see a few isolated horsemen making their way slowly across the fields towards the road—the flotsam and jetsam of a fast hunt. Tod noticed how the leaden sky seemed to be pressing down on the horizon, and knew that it would be snowing before long.

As he hurried on down the hill with his tireless, shambling strides, he saw an old farm laborer coming up the hill towards him pushing an ancient bicycle—Tod recognized him immediately as a regular follower of the Hunt, and hurried up to him.

"Seen hounds?" he asked.

"Aye," the old man replied, his face bright red from pedaling into the bitter wind, "Went through Selby Goss an' on towards Scarford."

"They're still hunting 'im then?" Tod asked eagerly, his heart beginning to beat again.

"Aye, an' I'll tell yer summat else, an' all. Young Durno's hunting 'em."

"Stephen?" Tod stopped in his tracks. "Where's Asher, then?"

"Went off on 'is own."

"What for?"

The old man shrugged and could tell him no more; after he had gone on up the hill. Tod stood trying to puzzle it out, then gave up and shambled forward again. Snow began to fall: sparsely at first, in small flakes that whirled past him without settling, but then in larger flakes that fell more and more thickly and began to silence his hurrying footsteps.

During the next hour Tod began to piece the story together from odd scraps of information picked up along the way. He learned that Asher had been seen—apparently alone, on an exhausted horse—heading across country towards Grimthorpe Hill. He heard, too, that hounds had killed on the outskirts of Scarford village, but it did not occur to him for a moment that this could have been Tag, for by this time he had guessed the reason for Asher's lonely hunt.

It was almost dark when Tod found the huntsman's horse: it was sheltering in the lee of a thick hedge, its head hanging miserably and trailing broken reins. Tod looked for tracks which might show him Asher's last direction but the falling snow had obliterated them and there was nothing to be seen. He threw his heavy coat over the shivering animal's loins and led it back towards the road. It was nearly eight o'clock before the Hunt horse-box met him leading the horse towards home and the groom told him that Asher had not returned.

There was no moon. It was impossible to search for the missing huntsman in the howling darkness, so Tod stayed with Cathie and Jenny at the kennels. A little later Stephen arrived, looking drawn and unhappy, and the four of them sat in the silent room waiting for the telephone to ring. Alone in his study, Kendrick was waiting, too. He had informed the police and telephoned dozens of people and now there was nothing else he could do. As he sat staring into the fire, thoughts were racing through his head—and one of them returned and returned to haunt him: the memory of his dismissal of Asher, that afternoon.

At five o'clock the next morning, Cathie and Jenny were both asleep; the girl was still, but Cathie struggled and whimpered in the armchair in front of the fire. Stephen sat upright on the old horse-hair sofa, with Jenny's head cradled in his lap. He looked up when Tod went across to the window and peered out at the eastern sky. The old man muttered something to himself, then turned to Stephen:

"Got yer car here?" he whispered hoarsely. Stephen nodded.

"Come on, then, lad."

Wordlessly, gently, Stephen lifted Jenny's head and laid it back on a cushion as he stood up. Tod made up the fire and together they crept out of the room and out of the silent house.

When Stephen pulled the car into a gateway and switched off the engine, distant trees were etched sharp and black against the lightening sky. The snow had stopped during the night, and the wind had dropped as well; no birds were singing in the spectral dawn and the only sound was the hushed tramp of their feet across the unblemished snow. Stephen saw the smoke of their breath in the crystalline air . . . *If we find him he'll be dead,* he thought suddenly.

As the daylight crept up the sky, first dimming and then extinguishing the stars, they searched along the lee of hedges and in the ditches, moving slowly towards the humped mass of Grimthorpe

Hill. Tod was silent and apparently absorbed in the search. Looking at him, Stephen tried to fathom the old man's feelings: he seemed so calm and unafraid. A vision of startling clarity flashed across Stephen's mind of the huntsman's body, stiff and gray beneath its coverlet of snow—he shivered, suddenly and violently. Tod turned and looked at him inquiringly. Stephen wanted to say *I'm all right*, but what he actually said was:

"I did love him, Tod."

The old man grinned, sardonic goat-teeth showing mockingly beneath the tangled moustache.

"Don't write 'im off too easy," he muttered, then looked ahead again, as though nothing had been said. Stephen tried to speak to him again after that, but Tod seemed not to hear: the young man had the impression that his senses were tuned in to some other frequency, and he was listening . . .

They climbed the lower slopes of Grimthorpe Hill and stopped at the edge of the spinney. It was almost full daylight, but still there was no sound anywhere, until Tod spoke:

"You go up that side," he said pointing, "and I'll go up here. We'll meet at the top and go down the far side."

He watched Stephen walking away from him, then turned towards the spinney. He heard the faint whisper of snow falling from an overladen branch, then silence again. He walked forward into the sparse undergrowth and started climbing steadily towards the Grimthorpe badger setts.

His eyes must have seen the fox standing at the mouth of the cave seconds before his mind grasped the information and stopped him in his tracks. Tag stood like a statue, less than twenty yards away, gazing calmly down at him, the white dash over his eye showing clearly against the darkness of the cave. Tod had no idea how long they stood like that, but it was a long time ... then the fox turned and melted silently away into the undergrowth. The old man gazed into the dimness of the wood, seeking a last glimpse of Tag: saw a flicker of russet between the trees, and then no more. "I'll look after yer, son," he said softly, then turned again to face the cave-mouth, black and forbidding, above him on the hillside.

He knew that Asher might be there, yet something made him hesitate before climbing the last few yards and entering the mystery of the cave-mouth. His ancient, pagan soul was trembling away from—*something* ... some presence, or hidden power ... then he pulled himself together with an effort and made himself walk on up the slope. When he stopped at the cave-mouth, the short hairs on the back of his neck were prickling.

A sound from inside the cave set his heart pounding ... he heard it again: a long-drawn-out, tremulous whimper—and suddenly he knew who it must be, and the fear fell away from his mind like a sloughed skin.

"Merlin!" he called, "Here, Merlin!"

But, to his surprise, the old hound failed to appear. Puzzled, Tod bent forward and entered the gloom of the cave, screwing his eyes shut to allow them to adjust to the darkness ... when he opened them again, he found he could see reasonably well, so he began peering round the cave.

He went suddenly still and silent as he saw the huddled shape, no more than a yard from where he stood. As his eyes became still more accustomed to the gloom, he was able to make out the indistinct shape of Merlin: lying beside his master, with his head resting on the huntsman's chest—and at that moment the old hound whimpered again: a long, tremulous whine that quavered down towards silence and ended in a faint query of tortured breath ... It was this outpouring of Merlin's grief that told the old man of Asher's pain; in the cold stillness that met his questioning fingers moments later, he found Asher unconscious but still alive.

For a little while Tod knelt over the huntsman's body, looking down at it calmly while Merlin lay huddled beside him. The old man's thoughts and emotions seemed to hang suspended in a globe of perfect stillness. The greenskeeper shook Asher and his eyelids fluttered as he awoke, cold and exhausted from exposure. Tod breathed his relief deeply, and found his lungs filled with air touched by the peace of Asher's survival and the joy of Tag's loyalty to his life-long friend.

That is how Stephen found them, nearly an hour later, after a frantic search across the empty hillside. He, too, was struck dumb by the fact of Asher's survival—but his silence was the hiding of confusion beneath a cloak of disbelief, while the old man's was a peaceful stillness to which he had simply surrendered.

Together they carried the huntsman out into the brilliant daylight and covered him with their overcoats. Then Stephen set off on the long walk to the road, while the old man and the foxhound stayed with Asher.

It was while Tod was rearranging the coats that he noticed the fine golden-red hairs that were mixed with the tan and white ones, all down the front of Asher's hunting-coat—he leaned closer for a better look, then realized with a shock that they were the fox's: Tag had huddled with Merlin to keep Asher warm and alive through the freezing night.

Sitting beside Asher's body, waiting for Stephen to return with a stretcher-party, Tod pieced together the story of Asher's long night, and the crucial role played by the two animals in his bitter struggle against death . . . he thought of the bright, generous spirit of the foxhound, who learned to love two friends when he was young, and never once swerved from that love and the unquestioning loyalty that went with it . . . and he thought of the strange paradox of the hunted fox, pursued relentlessly to his final refuge, sharing the sleep of exhaustion with his would-be executioner . . . and he thought, too, of Asher: gentle, tormented Asher, who loved both the hounds and the quarry they hunted . . . who tried always to deal fairly, judge wisely, speak truthfully and avoid self-esteem . . . who, loving, gave little enough of himself, it is true—yet took nothing in return . . . who was strong enough to be kind, and wise enough to be silent . . . and who lived—suffered—trying hard to do the right thing.

The old man's thoughts returned to his recurring vision of Asher's long night in the cave: unconscious and helpless, with only the warm bodies of the two animals huddled close against chest and abdomen to stand between him and death . . .

Tod looked at Merlin, his head still resting in silent, open-eyed devotion on the huntsman's chest; then he shook his head and sighed.

What a bit of luck, he thought: *He could no more destroy Tag than kill his own child.*